COLETTE R. HARRELL

LATER

INTENTIONAL
entertainment

Published and Distributed by
Intentional Entertainment, LLC

ISBN: 979-89862851-1-5 (paperback)
ISBN: 979-8-9862851-0-8 (ebook)

Library of Congress Control Number: 2022913378

Book Cover Design: Ana Grigoriu-Voicu, Books-Design.com
Interior Design: Jessica Tilles, TWASolutions.com

*To my mother, Dorothy E. Ford, who understands
that sometimes, time is all we have.*

*And my husband, Larry H. Harrell, who gave me
his time along with his heart.*

Acknowledgments

This has been a tough two years for most, and I can honestly proclaim I survived by God's grace and his specially assigned angels. I was challenged physically, mentally, spiritually, and emotionally. There were days when I didn't know if I wanted to make it, but the sun came up anyway. If you've never experienced what I'm talking about—let the testimony of my mouth assure you that God has you even in your darkest hour.

I want to thank my husband, Larry, who was my rock each and every day. He couldn't take a day off, and he didn't. This man was steadfast and unmovable when so many couldn't be located.

During an idea session with my daughter and her significant other, *Later* was created. Thank you, Melissa and Darryl, for allowing me to throw ideas out in brainstorming sessions.

I want to thank my son, Langston, and my grandsons, Halton and Henson, who stayed close and personal. Their love flowed richly over me.

I also want to thank the following people who held me up:

Dr. Norma McLauchlin and my Chosen Pen Family—they've become so dear and made North Carolina my second home. Lasheera Lee kept me on my toes as a friend and agent. Pam Bailey who never stopped exhibiting friendship at its finest. Family friend Mike J. Roebuck who held up my husband as he held me. Delrita Parks who trusts God in all things. Stephanie Bridges who encouraged me to embrace my business every step of the way. Shelia Faye Renfroe, we ride till the wheels fall off. And so many other friends and family members, I love you all.

This book is about God's timing and that your delay does not mean you've been denied. It's just coming . . . *Later*.

Prologue

We've been here a long time, me and the other shacks. We started out long ago as log cabins. The occupants spoke prayers of hope over shallow grunts as they flexed hardened muscles to build us strong. Then after backbreaking days in the tobacco fields, they made our dirt floors and grass-mixed-mud walls. Our wooden chimneys and brick hearths were the heart of our homes. It was a one-size-fits-all room, where they nursed their aches and caressed their wounds.

It wasn't all bad. We could sometimes smile as they made babies in a fevered pitch, good groans of satisfaction rolling through the air and out the window. Then we would rejoice, whispering up and down the quarters that it was a good night.

That's how we used to talk to each other, back and forth through the howling of the winds or the gentle flow of a breeze. There were days we'd moan with the pain of our inhabitants, who were too tired from the grueling work to tend to our needs. Took us a while to decide what to call them . . . inhabitants, occupants, residents? We never could decide. Inconsistency was a malevolent characteristic we all endured. They never owned us. Just stayed a bit while they could. And, to be fair, they tried to keep us up. Oh, we got a hit and a lick of mud before the winter winds blew, but it was meager labor. Neglect was easy when profits were the owner's goal, and the fields were a harsh partner.

Years later, our dilapidated wooden logs would be eaten, digested by termites with fat bellies. Laid out in a row like coffins after the war. No hero's welcome for all we had endured. We whisper about it even now through broken windows that no longer hold our secrets. Others may think it's the wind howling, but those are our screams, held captive for years while we watched, waited, and hungered for habitation. Hungered while generations of slaves and sharecroppers had nothing to share . . . No more to give. Watched as Big Mama, who carried large pots of water to an iron tub, whittled down to nothing but bones as she lay on my dirt floor every evening, moaning in pain . . . waiting for change.

At first, new folk moved in when others gave up. And each added their blood and mud to slather yawning cracks and holes to keep the walls standing. Our neglect could not be camouflaged, but the Missus, she'd hang little bits of cloth on the window and add dandelion flowers to a tin can, hoping to add a touch of pretty.

Just a mile away, majestically, stood the big house. Cruel in its taunting of us as it was painted and scrubbed and loved on—even by those who hated it. It defied the old man's hands of time. *Tick, tick, tick.*

Every inch forward of its hand proclaimed a litany.

Poor folk got it bad. Poor folk got it bad. We chanted out of walls with exposed spaces.

We tried hard, this holding on of bones. We struggled when it rained; our roofs had few shingles, more wet than dry, more holes than substance. The hearth hungered. No remembered warmth dwelled here.

I saw the change when the doors fell, one by one. Then it was the disrespect—no knock—just folk walking inside without a "Come in and sit a spell" invite. No longer hardworking folk, slaves, sharecroppers, but now, drug-addled brains lighting up and dozing off. A few of us went up in flames while others watched and bled rusted nails.

One of us lost our balance, teetered . . . and fell over. Me and the other shacks yelled back and forth about it.

No reason to whisper now. No one to listen.

We were ready. Maybe some child could rumble through the wood and find a piece left good enough to make a kite and fly me down the street.

Free.

Chapter One

1859

It was 1859, and the tips of fingers and noses were suffering. It was the beginning of what slaves at the Benson Plantation felt was a bitter, cold Tennessee winter. In reality, it was a brisk thirty-five degrees, but with thin-bare coats and a lack of gloves or proper shoes, their perception of bitter cold was skewed. Nevertheless, one of the places outside of the towering, big house with the enormous Roman pillars and its kitchen that held any real warmth was the smithy. And as snowflakes trickled and turned wet as they hit the ground, the clang of the red-hot anvil sang across the air.

Clang. Clang. Clang.

No upcoming approach could be heard in the clamor of the hammer pounding away. Then, with small hands clutching her threadbare coat to her chest, a vision of beauty came flying into view.

She slid and was almost upended as she called out, "Papa, Papa, I gots to tell ya."

John's hammer continued to ring as he placed a new shoe on the hoof of Massa's favorite horse.

Face smudged with ash, twelve-year-old Junie looked up from the corner where he sat huddled, perched on an overturned bucket. He looked down at the mud, where his stick and foot had quickly scratched and smeared out the words he was practicing.

"Doggon' it, Sari girl, I was figuring letters! You beat all. Make some noise, why don't cha? Sneaking up like a possum trying to get past a po' hungra fox."

Gasping, the twenty-year-old Sarah, otherwise known as Sari, squinted her eyes, furtively glanced behind her shoulder, and with her hand on her waist, proclaimed, "Watch yo' mouth, boy chile. If I could catch ya, so can others. You know we neva cipher in daylight, Junie—neva!"

Vexed, he peered at his ruined words. "Shush, gal. Nighttime too hard. Gotta catch the light while I can. Candlelight too dim. Can't see if my letters is straight 'nuff." Junie stood and walked over to his sister, waiting.

Eyes blinking, Sari exhaled, started to speak, and then paused.

"Well, girl? You callin', and I's here," John Benson said with a grimace that altered his usually gentle, brown face.

Junie knew his father loved him some Sari, nick-named by his beloved "gone to glory" mother, but his sister was prone to fits of drama. Therefore, she never quite grew to the sedate name of Sarah, so Sari she remained and acted to all. He believed her fits came from being up in the big house all the time. Massa's missus was right theatrical. He heard tell through Cinda that they used up the smelling salts quite regular because of her goings-on.

John was a man who was average in stature but stood tall. Sari and Junie looked up to him and imagined his five-foot-nine stature as a towering six feet. Even when they saw their father bend to the will of others, there was steel in his eyes that let them know his spirit was not beaten.

"Papa, I hear Massa say war comin'. He say if that there Lincoln fella run for office, they gon' take us away, and we gon' starve. We ain't gon' have no place to go, and I don't wanna be more hungra, Papa." Sari huffed as she pulled her apron hard around her hand, winding it further up her body.

Junie looked at his papa and waited for what he would say. He already knew what he had been hearing for the last month, that it was time to go. Junie had shared every word with Papa. They had always planned according to the voice and sometimes just the urgings Junie had in his spirit. Over Junie's young life, both the urgings and the voice proved to be infallible. When he was just three years old, the old root woman, Betunde, told his papa and mama that they needed to heed Junie's mumblings, even when it didn't make sense. The miracle of first Junie's mother, then Junie hearing from the divine voice moved Betunde. Betunde came to know the Lord better than the plantation's visiting reverend. What was once her root work became the root of the tree of life. The mumblings Betunde told them to note had become clear sentences and instructions by Junie's fourth birthday. Betunde had since been laid to rest, along with his beloved mama. However, Betunde's words were never laid down nor buried. Instead, they became hallowed wisdom they all lived by.

Papa decided they wouldn't reveal much to Sari. It wasn't that they didn't trust her, but she was overly excited and had the habit of oversharing when she was overwhelmed. And she tended to succumb to fits of worry easily. Knowing their plans derived from the voice would surely send her into overdrive. But voice or not, even thinking about leaving Benson Plantation would be an act of betrayal, and the consequences were ten lashes. Massa then made bad worse because he mandated that coarse salt and red pepper were rubbed into the mangled, bleeding flesh after each whipping. You could hear in each cabin the grunts of agony and bewildered cries as the solution intermingled with the blood flowing freely from each slash. Some folk might say that Benson folk had it good, as opposed to slaves on the neighboring plantation. They heard tell of hot tar being poured onto the open wounds of whipped slaves and then set on fire at the Plessy place.

Junie had never been whipped. Sari and his father, John, had never been whipped. But Junie, like all the other slaves on the Benson Plantation, had witnessed beatings. It was mandated that every slave, young and old, feeble or sick, attend the public whippings. Many who were whipped were never the same. Some just up and died. Once, Duke, a big strapping buck, got whipped for moving too slow for the overseer. That man got so angry that he had Duke tied to the old pine oak and whipped him till Duke forgot who he was. Now, Duke permanently worked slow, shuffled, and drooled. Nobody wanted to end up like Duke.

Papa said a scared man wasn't right-minded. That overseer was so scared of big, strong Duke that he had to bring him down when he failed to bow low and fast enough. Papa shared that anxious men were the most dangerous, and most white gentry was fearful of lots of things, even poor white folk, like being poor was a disease they didn't want to catch.

The overseer was fired due to him messing with Massa's property, but Duke still had an addled brain.

John Benson was the blacksmith on the plantation. He worked from sunup to sundown. He shoed horses, repaired wagons, or anything else needing ironworks. He was hired out around the town and neighboring lands. He had an affinity for anything mechanical. For the last twelve years, he could be seen in the Benson Plantation's wagon pulled by two robust horses going up and down the road, plying his wares for Massa Benson. He made the Benson Plantation good money and won favor from neighboring plantations, farms, and county folk. He was known to have a fine touch with steel and iron. And could just as easily make a decorative scroll of iron as he could to create tools and fastenings for doors and barns. The neighbors loved his work, especially those who didn't have to go into town for help. As such, he had more privileges than most. There was hope in those privileges.

Junie had a knack for numbers and inventions that made crops more bountiful, and he could hear tell of a stock the Massa shared with him and tell if it was going to prosper as an investment. He had helped make the Benson Plantation wealthy. Massa Benson would always say that the labor of the sinner is laid up for the righteous to get wealth. He then would say, with evil in his eye, that all slaves were sinners, cursed by Noah's son, Ham. And as much as God spoke to Junie, He stayed silent on that one. It didn't sound like the God he knew, but Junie got right discombobulated when the reverend held the slaves' church services on Sunday. He never understood that the God they quoted never felt like the Divinity who spoke to him.

Picking up his hammer again, John swung it through the air sending out a large clang. "Don't cha worry nothing 'bout no war, Sari girl. Go on back 'fore they see ya missin' from de kitchen."

"Yes'm, Papa. Sho' be glad when Sunday next come. Christmas Day gon' be some good eatin'." Sari slid backward toward the door, her rambling mind already on to something else.

Junie shared a look with his father as John shook his head, turned, and continued shoeing the horse. Finally, he sat back down on his overturned bucket and placed his stick in the mud he had created as his blackboard when they heard Sari call out. Junie, legs stretching, flew to the alcove opening, and he braced his back against the wall to peek around the door.

Her voice five octaves higher, Sari gushed, "Hey 'there, Massa. Just asking Papa if he want us to bring him his supper. On a count, he workin' so hard for ya today, don't want to slow him down none."

Eyebrows bunched like a caterpillar streaking across his forehead, Jacob Benson groused, "Not your concern, gal. Go on and get back to the house. Your Missus or Cinda might need ya."

"Yes, Suh, Massa. I's goin' now." Her long legs spread as she hurried to the big house's kitchen, calling back, "Missus love her afternoon tea."

Junie was lightning quick moving back to his place.

John nodded to Junie, who had moved his bucket over the scratching lines in the dirt.

Standing erect from his task, John bent his head when Jacob Benson entered the smithy. Jacob's piercing green eyes lasered on his stallion. "How's he looking, John boy? He going to be ready to race come spring?"

"Yes, suh. I believes so. Old Silas say this gon' do it."

"Good. I got races to win." He then tipped back his hat. "Now, I got two places that need some work. First, you go on out to the Plessy place. They needs some iron fastenings for their barn. Then go on to the Johnson place and fix the carriage. Dag blasted thang almost kilt Ms. Margaret when the wheel fell off." He then yanked his hat clear off his head, slapping his thigh. "And only do what I tell you. Jedidiah Plessy got a bad habit of trying to add to your list when you get there, but then conveniently forget to pay me."

At Jacob's last statement, a tiny tick formed in the corner of John's left eye. "Yes, suh. Be right on it."

Jacob looked over his shoulder as he twirled his hat in his hands. "I see you back there, Junie. You don't have no work waiting on you?"

"No, suh. Filled up all the water pots, dumped all the chamber pots, and gathered the eggs and two chickens for Cinda. She said I could go for a bit unless you'se had need of me. You needs me?"

Jacob spit snuff right by Junie's foot. He flinched but dared not move it an inch. "Well, now, boy, if I did need you, you wouldn't have been there, now, would you?" He used his hat to point toward the smithy door. "So, go on and git."

Junie walked outside of the smithy and fell back against the smithy wall to eavesdrop on the rest of what Massa Jacob Benson wanted with his father. He could always tell when Massa wasn't finished spouting like a fountain.

"Listen you here, John. Just 'cause you and them youngins of yours ain't been whipped don't mean I won't whip 'em. You hear me, boy? Thangs getting a little too loose around c'here. I don't like it, coming and going like they got the right. This going to stop!"

John hung his head and nodded.

"And another thang. Don't cha be paying no mind to any talk you hear in town, and don't you be bringing it back to this c'here plantation. You hear me, boy?"

Head already bowed, John stooped more, then stood still. "Yes, suh. I hear's ya."

"All right then. You've always been a good Negra, John. So don't go making me change my mind 'bout cha being a good Negra."

"No, suh, Massa."

Not wanting to get caught, Junie ran as fast as he could on the frost-covered ground into the kitchen. There was always work to be done, and he better be caught doing it.

The kitchen was two stories high, about seven-hundred square feet wide, and separate from the big house. It stayed toasty warm, which was welcomed in the winter and woefully miserable in the summer. The smells could be overpowering in such close range, but it kept the Benson family from having to smell day-old food, a too-hot house, or risk a fire to their main home. On the first floor, Cinda cooked sumptuous meals for the Benson Plantation; on the second floor, she, Gussie, and Gussie's daughter, Tulip, had pallets for sleeping and cubbies for their belongings with nails in the wall to hang their clothes.

Cinda smiled with warmth when she saw Junie enter the kitchen. "Bells and horns, Junie. You be c'here right on time, and I needs sometin' from de cellar. Brang me up five apples and ten potatoes, and grab me a side of pork. Massa want pork roast on da morrow."

Junie nodded, grabbed the sack sitting in the corner for that purpose, and ran out the door to the root cellar building right next door. Once he entered the building, he went down the stairs of the dank-smelling dwelling, lay on his belly in front of the first pit, pulled potatoes out of the sand, and placed them in the sack. He then stood and walked down to more pits until he reached the one that held only bushels of apples. Massa Benson was partial to apples and loved him a cobbler, pie, applesauce, or some kind of pork garnished with cinnamon apples. Junie lay down again and reached down until he brought forth the apples Cinda wanted. He placed everything Cinda asked for in the sack and then added a few extra things in his inner coat pocket.

He then stood and climbed up the steps and walked over to the many smoked meats hanging from hooks in the ceiling. Next to the hanging meat were dried beans, corn to be ground into meal, and under them, shucks of grain. Junie took down the requested side of pork but took nothing there for himself. The overseer's wife checked the inventory in the root cellar regularly, and while she never could tell if any root vegetables were missing, she counted all the meat and checked it against the missus's daily menu. Junie was smart enough only to take the items Cinda was cooking for the big house meals. He would then transfer them to their storage root pit in their cabin's dirt floor.

"It's not thieving. It's payment." Junie spoke to the dank air and hoped the voice heard him.

It would be hard to go through with their plans in the early winter, but one advantage was hiding things in their oversized coats. Junie's coat was a hand-me-down, too big for him but perfect for hiding his stash. The other winter benefit was that nighttime came early, giving them more time to run and less daylight to follow. They also didn't have to contend with soggy land, mosquitoes, and such on their journey. The voice said go, and they had used every bit of each day to prepare. Papa and Junie knew time was running out.

Going out the cellar door and into the kitchen building, he saw Sari sitting at the table kneading bread. They smiled at each other, Sari's accompanied with a saucy wink. They were different in looks. Her leafy-green eyes, long, brown-auburn tipped curls, a heart-shaped face with her pert nose, and almond-toasted complexion was in sharp contrast to his cinnamon-hued eyes, warm brown skin, and broad forehead and nose. Both were attractive people, but the observers' hearts measured beauty. Some folks, like the missus, called Junie ugly because his looks spoke to a land far away. But both Cinda and Sari assured him often he was a handsome boy and would be a fine, strapping man.

As though looks mattered when what a man needed was a broad back and fit mind . . .

Junie didn't put much worry in his looks. He knew his mind worked right well. But he worried about his Sari girl every day. The only thing that kept her safe was that Massa had an uncommon soft spot for her, but Junie knew it wouldn't be long before Massa bred her. She was over the age, and her beauty was well known. Massa had turned down offers to buy her or just to bed her, but he said no with a gleam in his eye like she was a Christmas turkey not quite ready for the table . . . but almost.

Sighing, Junie said, "Cinda, Massa still going to his mama's for Christmas?"

Cinda clapped the flour off her hands as she moved around the kitchen in sync with her tasks. "Yes, Junie. Third time ya done ask me such. Why?"

"Uh, I'se hopin' he don't make me go, that's all."

"He say you staying here, Junie."

Sari's neck swiveled back and forth between the two. "Missus say she might take me. Ain't that nice, Junie?"

Startled and eyes wide, Junie stuttered over his words. "Y-y-you don't need to go, Sari."

"But I neva get off this c'here place. I so too will go."

Junie saw Cinda purse her lips and was glad when she said, "Baby girl, sometime, home is the onliest place you's safe. And that there might not be true most time."

Sari's face fell, and her eyes glazed. "You hear tell I can't go, Junie?"

Junie knew she was referring to how he heard the voice and how, over the years, that voice had kept them safe.

Do I lie? he wondered. "No, I ain't heard on this in particula. But, Sari, I know. Don't go."

Sari bit her lip and then gave a sharp nod of her head. "I think on it. But may not be my call, Junie. If Missus say, Massa do."

Junie sucked in his breath and turned his head so they couldn't read his face. On top of the anxiety for all his plans to come through, he was now extra worried.

Sari girl, just 'cause a thing got silk walls and padded don't mean it ain't a cage.

Chapter Two

Present

Lt. Colonel Zachary Trumble turned over in his bed and peeked at the alarm clock with one eye open. It was a little after five in the morning, and he knew it was time to rise and shine.

There was a time when I was already up and facing my squad, ready to meet the day. Civilian life makes you lazy.

Grasping his knees as he sat up, he yawned, stretched, and rubbed his six-pack stomach.

Is that fat? Man, am I getting a dad bod without the benefit of any kids?

As ex-Special Forces, he was used to being on assignment, adrenalin pumping, his body a weapon. On his job at Burstein Labs, his days were dull. It gave him too much time to sit and snack and wonder just what they really did there. He was paid a high six-figure salary to maintain what amounted to keeping the public out of their business. The corporate espionage he thought would be a problem was nonexistent because mainly, no one he knew, knew what Burstein Labs did . . . including himself.

Zachary swung his legs out of bed and moved his foot around in the dark, searching for his slipper. He tried to move silently so that he didn't disturb or, God forbid, wake, his wife, Sylvia. Not because he loved her so much that he wouldn't disturb her rest, but because to disturb her rest would bring on the wrath of a banshee. He didn't have it in him to go a full round with her before work. He had learned to maintain peace in small ways. One small way was to slip out of the house early and come home late. He held peace close, like a squirrel hoarding nuts for the winter. If he added enough small moments of peace, he might be able to turn them in to whoever ran the universe and score a whole night of silence.

"Slipping out?" Sylvia said in a dry voice.

Now she's reading minds? "Just being courteous, love."

Sylvia sat up and turned on the lamp, then said in a huff, "Don't need your manners; just need you to man up. Can you just try to be more *visible* at work? Show them what you can do. You're up for your annual review in a month. You want them to recognize your worth with a nice bonus."

Zachary withered, resembling a deflating balloon with a pinhole. *Here we go again.* "Sylvia, I make a ridiculous amount of money now for what I do. More than I ever thought I would. We're good."

"Ugggh! Must you be so mediocre? Do you *really* have zero ambition? You were Special Forces, for goodness' sake. You could be a mercenary making tons of money. But no—"

"—First of all, I left the military and my service to my country because of your mis—"

Clutching the pillow to her middle, she spewed, "Don't you say it. Uh-uh. No! If you had been here, then my stress—"

"*Your* stress? What about *my* stress? *I* lost a baby too. And I was only going to say, *if you would ever let me finish a thought*, I left the military under the *misguided* belief you needed me. But what you *really* needed was a bigger payday. And just because I don't measure success in dollars, don't call me mediocre."

"You major on minor, Zachary. I can't keep carrying you in this relationship." She rose from the bed and stomped into the enclosed suite bathroom.

Rubbing his hand down his face, he jabbed his fingers through his hair. "Here we go with this bull. How are *you* carrying *me*, and you don't even have a job, Sylvia? You haven't worked since I left the service."

"Don't you want to try again? Don't you want a baby? Huh? Well, I'm not bringing a child up in the poverty I was raised in. So *do* something, please!" she said as she yanked up her gown and sat on the toilet. Then looking up, she slammed close the bathroom door.

Zachary trudged out of the room, down the hall to the guest bath, and into the shower. It was just like Sylvia to wake up early, disturb his peace, and then make him work extra just to take a stupid shower. Zachary was getting fed up. His parents were married forty years. His brother had been married for ten years. He was thirty-two years old and had left a life he loved to be unhappy and shackled. He didn't want to divorce Sylvia, but the way things were going, he wouldn't have to make a move. *She* would divorce *him*.

Standing under the water that streamed down his face, his dimpled cheeks taut with stress, he remembered an auburn beauty running through the rain to catch a bus. She slipped right in front of him and into his arms. In their good days, he teased, she fell for him first. Home on leave, Zachary looked into the greenest eyes he had ever seen and fell in lust. When he was a boy, he dreamed about a girl with green eyes. Everything else faded to dark in his dreams, or maybe after time, everything else had faded away but the vivid eyes in his dream. Those eyes made an adolescent him want to rap about it, a teenager want to sing about it, so when as an adult, they fell into his arms, he was a goner.

Later, she told him, he had her at the uniform. She said she wanted a house full of kids, a house with a white picket fence, and only him. It was what Zachary needed to hear. He was tired of being the only soldier not getting mail from his one and only because he didn't have one. The longer he was gone from home, when he returned, the more everyone was paired up. Then they were paired up with children. People were working on their second homes, and he hadn't even purchased his first one.

Soaping up as steam swirled up around him, he remembered thinking that meeting Sylvia was the beginning of bliss . . .

Taking long strides as his size twelve feet ate up the pavement, a blur of checkered red and white flew past him. Before he could catch sight of what it was, it became a she who was launching knees bent into the pavement.

Stretching out, with military-honed instincts, Zachary was able to catch her around the waist and bring her to a full stand. Flipping her long, auburn hair out of her face, she smiled, her green eyes twinkling, and for him, the sun came out and shined.

Zachary slowly slid his muscled arms from around her waist and, as he released her, took an appropriate step back.

"Hi!" she said, and as her eyes roamed up and down his six-foot chiseled body, her smile widened.

"Hi, back," Zachary said, already knowing he would ask her out. "You good?"

Laughter like a bubbling brook flowed from her center. "Absolutely. You're a knight slaying dragons. Thank you for your service, Soldier."

Playing along, Zachary swept his hat from his head and swung his arm across his body as he bent over, tipping his hat as he went. "At your service, milady."

In a coquettish manner, she bit the bottom of her lip, batted her eyelashes, and in a sultry voice, said, "I like that. At ease, Soldier. I'd love to thank you properly, show my gratitude for your gallant rescue. Care to take a walk to the corner Starbucks for a latte, my treat?"

Zachary held out his arm, and she fit her red, work-roughened hand in the crook. Then embarrassed, she placed her coat-covered arm over her hand and squeezed.

Zachary had always admired the hard work of others, and her embarrassment of her rough hands made her vulnerability all the more attractive. Patting her coat sleeve, he said, "I'd be honored. I'm not a latte man, but your company and a strong coffee sound good."

Gently caressing his bicep, she chuckled. "Aren't you the sweetest? I'm Sylvia, by the way."

"Lt. Colonel Zachary Trumble, United States Army, glad to make your acquaintance, ma'am."

"Well, we'll certainly see about that," she said, her hips moving to a calypso beat as they strolled down the street.

Zachary had been alone so long that he thought God smiled on him that day with a green-eyed goddess, especially when, two hours later, their legs were tangled together in her Walmart sheets, and he sighed in satisfaction.

They dated for a year, but out of that year, he only saw her for a total of six weeks. He missed her. He missed the sex. She worked hard as a waitress and always complained about not being available for him the entire time he was home due to her hours. Special Forces had its privileges, but she needed to marry him to be with him on base.

On impulse, against his family's counsel, he got down on one knee, and they had a small ceremony in his parents' backyard, and Sylvia quit the restaurant and moved on base housing with him. It was her first time not having a roommate *and* living in a house.

She would cook him elaborate meals that were so bad, they both would laugh after one bite, order pizza, and make love all night. Now, she ordered in, or they ate out. She bought, and bought, and bought. The more he gave, the more she took. Their life together was one long roller coaster of revelations. She demanded to get her breasts done. He complied, but he was baffled by her need for more than he required. His biggest surprise was when she stopped making her beauty routine private. One night after a loud fight, he stopped in his tracks when she roughly lathered her face with goop, snatched off her eyelashes, and popped out jade-colored contacts. He was jolted awake to find his green-eyed goddess was a faded, brown-eyed gold digger.

Shutting off the water shut down his reminiscing. Zachary stepped out, patting himself dry. Wiping the fog from the mirror, he caught the frown on his face as he brushed back his brownish blond hair and got lost in the new grooves around his mouth. Sighing, he opened the medicine cabinet and took out a travel toothpaste and a spare toothbrush. He no longer knew where that Sylvia had gone. Or the love. Rinsing out his mouth, he thought maybe the actual question was if it had ever been real.

Because how did she start by making your heart sing, only to find out she was pantomiming like the fake pop group Milli Vanilli, and when the music stopped, you heard she was singing horribly off-key?

Pulling up to Burstein Labs, Zachary stared at the structure. The building was out in the rural area of town and looked like a farm equipment warehouse, down to the silo and tractor in the nearby field.

A couple of farms surrounded it, but you never saw any of the neighbors venture over. The underground parking lot housed the staff's parking; only the lowest-level staff was assigned to aboveground parking. It was a puzzle. And after three years of working there, Zachary was not buying half of what they were selling.

Inside, men and women in white lab coats robotically walked in and out of elevators and offices. Most didn't speak, and it was a cold, sterile work environment. Checking in for any issues that may have occurred there the night before, Zachary called his second into his office.

A short knock and the door opened. Tom Simmons, his assistant chief of security, sauntered in. He flopped down in his chair and rocked it to and fro. "Nothing to report, boss. Usual stuff. Quiet and boring. All personnel checked in on time and are ready to check out."

"I guess it would be wrong to want a little excitement around here. Everything runs pretty much like clockwork."

"Well, get this. One thing did happen. Several of the lab coats came in, and then all left within the same hour. Took a caravan out of here like they were being chased."

Zachary stood. "Tom, that is something unusual happening. Why didn't you call me?"

"Because nothing happened. They came, they went. Nothing here changed. And no one said a word to me."

Zachary sucked his teeth in disgust. "Okay, man, you can take off. See you tonight."

Tom jumped out of his chair and gave Zachary a military salute. Zachary didn't bother to return it since he knew Tom had never served. He was just somebody's relative who had one year on the police force before he was hired. After that, he did as little as possible, as much as possible. It's why Zachary moved him to nights, where even less happened.

Grabbing his phone, Zachary buzzed his boss. He was glad he was also an early arrival most days. "Hello, sir, is everything all right? I received a report that there was some unusual activity last night." Then in eagerness, Zachary asked, "Is there any assistance I can provide you?"

"Zachary, my boy, on top of things as always. You may actually be able to be of assistance later. I need you to put a team together of our best security people. I'll tell you more later."

"Roger that, sir. Should we be ready to roll out?"

"No, no. You should be ready for what's rolling in," he said and hung up.

Zachary rubbed his hands together. He was finally going to see some action. His daily inactivity was stifling after being sent to jungles, deserts, and countries too small to find on a map. On top of feeling that something was not quite right, with all the locked areas and signs to unauthorized personnel to keep out, maybe now he'd see what really went on at Burstein Labs.

Picking up his phone to call his best men to his office, he hesitated. *What or who is coming?*

Chapter Three

1859

Junie sat at the big wooden table. He ran his hands over the cuts and marks as though his fingers could memorize each groove.

"Cat yankin' on your tongue, youngen?" Cinda asked as she easily lifted the copper pot and hung it on a hook from the iron rod.

"No, ma'am, just wishing thangs were so."

Cinda moved with a slow purpose as she leaned over and caught Junie's chin in her large hand. "Baby boy, you so special. The angels blew kisses in your ears and rub noses with you when you was born."

"You was there?"

"Sho' was! Chile, you fought your way out." She cackled as she held her fists in front of her with a fighter's stance. "'Bout put your mammy under, you did." Cinda's eyes drifted shut as she thought back to those times. "She was a fighter, dat one. She was smart and pretty and loved y'all like biscuits sopping up molasses. Dat stick to ya, love."

"That's what Papa say. He say my mammy had grit."

"Yes, sir. You gots it too. Now, Sari girl, she dat word dat I heard Massa say a lot . . . content."

Junie rolled his eyes. "My sister don't know no betta. She Missus's pet, her only having boys, and she Massa prize her being white-folk pretty."

"You notice dat, did ya? You see too much, boy. Head so full of grown folk bizness, you been less a child den most."

Cinda looked back and forth and wrapped a thick slice of ham in cheesecloth. She placed it first in a pail and put a piece of burlap over it. Then she added corn bread and cheese on top.

"Junie, take this down to your papa." Junie gave a slight nod as he grabbed the pail and made his way to leave. "Your papa a mighty fine man. Mayhap someday he get over ya mama."

Junie left. He understood some things were left unspoken. Papa told him what happens between a man and woman was just that . . . between a man and woman.

Junie had thought on it and understood his papa couldn't freely love Cinda 'cause he wasn't free to love himself. It was a hard truth for Junie to learn, and his papa had accepted. Papa had struggled with feeling powerless with his first love. He had vowed not to love that way again. The pain was too great.

Junie kept his coat cinched closed with a cord as he hurried to the smithy so his papa could eat. There was enough daily sacrifice without him lollygagging.

Clang. Click. Clang. Click.

"Papa, it works!" Junie said as he watched his father test out the spring attached to the board.

"It does. Now, all I got to do is take some of Massa's springs he had me work into his carriage and get them to Doc Wingate's."

"Papa, there's news. Sari said she going to Massa's mama's for Christmas with the missus."

"You didn't say anything to her, did ya?"

"No, sir. Sari like running water. Her words carry over to evabody."

"Good, good."

"I'se been studyin' on it, though. And if Dr. Wingate can do us one more good deed?"

"He'll do it for ya, boy. Said he neva seen such a fine mind as you'rn."

"His mama from up North. Dr. Wingate be different. Here's what I'm thinking . . ." Junie said as he hunched over and, in a conspiratorial tone, shared his plan.

The darkened room was stuffy, even with Junie waving a fan over the missus's head. Tiny beads of perspiration dotted her forehead as the doctor asked her to breathe in deeply.

"Oh dear. Are you sure, Dr. Wingate? I don't feel that bad."

"Well, my dear, you look to be melancholy. Are you sure you haven't had a cough, dear?" Dr. Wingate asked as he patted the missus's plump, soft hand.

"Maybe a little. Oh dear, yeah, I must rest. Jacob will be devastated that I'm unable to travel with him. We were leaving on the morrow with Christmas just a few days away."

"It's best to be safe, my dear. It's a two-day ride, and with someone as delicate as you, we can't be too careful."

"Boy, instead of just standing there, keep fanning. I feel faint," Virginia Benson whimpered.

"Ms. Virginia, I'm leaving this syrup for you to take three times a day. Just a teaspoon, now. It's potent."

A now reedy voice answered between engineered coughs. "Thank you so much, Donald. This is so vexing. I did so want to accompany Jacob to his brother's. Their Lucy makes the best food. Cinda is good, but Lucy is better."

"I'm sure Mr. Benson will be as sad to leave you behind as you are to stay. His mama is going to miss you too, I'm sure."

"Ha! Not likely, and that's the rainbow at the end of this storm. Boy, please, go fetch your massa."

"Yes'em," Junie said and placed the fan in Sari's hand as he ran out of the room.

Junie then fell back against the wall by the door to eavesdrop. He was getting good at it, but it was a stealth operation, and he didn't know how much longer he had the temperament for it.

Missus Benson waved her hand in front of her and dabbed her handkerchief across her forehead. It was a well-worn gesture, seen by all on numerous occasions. "It's so hard to get the right help. My Jacob says he's smarter than most Negras, but I can't see it. Now, Sari is smart and sweet. Such a good companion."

Clearing his throat, Dr. Wingate murmured, "They are a peculiar people."

Mrs. Benson scrunched her nose and tittered behind her hand. "Truth be told, I abhor my mother-in-law. She is so hard to please. I'm so glad she decided she preferred Jacob's brother, Worth's wife, to me. Let her run her crazy. I will miss seeing my boys on Christmas Day, but they'll be here after," she said as her voice drifted off.

Dr. Wingate nodded his head in sympathy.

"Sari girl, put that fan down. Get my bed ready for me."

Sari went to the bed to straighten it and put a hot pan rolled in fabric at the bottom to warm up the bed for when the night would soon chill.

Dr. Wingate cleared his throat. "You are so lucky to have so many servants to help you through this time. Why, my one gal, Delia, has up and gotten sick on me. It is right inconvenient."

"Oh my, you don't say?"

"Yes. Well, your girl here, Sari, is young and strong. You are so blessed, madam."

"She is a strong girl."

"I was just telling them at the Plessy place how benevolent you are, kindhearted and generous to a fault. They were quite impressed. No one gives as much as you, Ms. Virginia. A true saint."

"Oh, the Plessy place? You were telling them all about me?" Ms. Virginia sat up straighter in her chair. "I do try to help those less fortunate. I tell you what, Donald. Take Sari with you. She's a good girl and strong, as you say."

"Oh, thank you, Ms. Virginia, but I wouldn't want to put you out any. This grippe is something awful this season. I am running ragged trying to keep up."

"Well, now, we have over three hundred folk on this property, and Cinda and her girl, Gussie, will work just fine for me. I can let you have Sari this week only."

Junie peeked in and saw Sari's eyes go wide. *Hush, Sari, don't ya say it.*

"But, ma'am, what if we was to send Gussie? Ya not well. Ya goin' needs me."

Turning her head sharply, Ms. Virginia looked over at Sari with a piercing scowl on her face. "Not talking to you, gal. Don't interrupt when your betters are talking. You will spend Christmas at the doctor's house helping him with whatever he asks for. Are we clear?"

Curtseying, Sari said, "Yes, Missus."

Junie took off, knowing there was no more to be gleaned from the conversation. He did as most youth and galloped down the staircase. Unfortunately, at the end of the winding stairs stood Rubin, head of all things big house.

As usual, the scowl on his face was ever-present when a slave was in front of him.

"You are not allowed to run downstairs, boy. Tomorrow, you will come here before your morning chores begin and scrub de's stairs clean. Every single one of dem."

"Missus sent me for Massa," Junie said. He hated running into old Rubin. He didn't like anybody but Massa, Missus, and they two boys who were away in school.

"Den what you standing here talkin' to me for, boy?"

Frowning, Junie knocked on the den door.

"What is the matter with you, boy? Did I not say don't bother me none?" Jacob screamed through the door.

"It Junie, Massa," he said as he slowly opened the door.

"Come here, boy. Let me ask you something. Is a shipping line that carries thousands of dollars of goods in two months, has been in business for twenty years, is the second generation, and is looking to add three more ships to their line of ten ships a good investment?"

Eyes blinking rapidly against his nerves, Junie asked, "Goods or people goods, Massa?"

Knocking over the ink well, Jacob stood. "You getting smart, boy? You questioning me, 'bout my business dealings, boy?"

"Nah, sir, Massa. But if war coming and peoples not gon' be—"

The slap came so hard and swift that Junie was lifted off his feet and then fell to his knees. The next kick was swift and hard against his small, wiry chest.

"Rubin!" Jacob thundered from his office.

Swift feet shuffles could be heard coming down the hall. Then suddenly, the door opened, and Rubin took in the scene before him. "Yes, Massa, sir."

"Remove him from my view. Perhaps I will see him after my return for a real whipping. I must think on it."

"Yes, sir," Rubin said as he picked up Junie from the floor and pushed him out of the office.

Jacob called out to Rubin as he went to close the door. "No meals for him for the next two days. See to it."

Rubin softly closed the door. "Go home, boy. Be back here in the morrow early and get to scrubbing the stairs. I'll be lettin' Cinda know, no food for ya. Now get."

Junie stumbled out of the big house. His face and chest were throbbing, and his back ached. He was stunned. He had never been hit so viciously before. He knew now just a little of what other slaves had endured. Limping home, he knew; yes, it was *definitely* time for them to go.

Junie then smiled. He never did tell Massa that Missus wanted him. He 'spect she was going to be real mad when Massa finally got up dere.

The wind whistled through the door as Junie came in and closed it behind him. It got dark early in the winter, and John was already sitting down waiting for him. His eyebrows rose when he saw the bruising beginning to show on Junie's face.

"What don' happen'd?"

Junie glanced away from his father. He knew he couldn't do nothing about ol' Massa, and he hated making him feel worse than he already did. "Nothin'."

"Don' you lie to me, Junie. I might can't do nothin', but I can be dere for ya."

Junie ran into his father's large, brawny arms and sobbed. "It was my fault, Papa. I forgot my place, Papa. Spoke on thangs best left unsaid."

"Ya speak truth, Junie?"

"As I's knows it."

Nodding once, John stood and sighed. "We best be going over this plan one more time before Sari girl come in." He opened the door and broke a bit of ice off the overhanging roof. Then he placed it in a rag and handed it to Junie, who put it on his face.

"It worked, Papa. Dr. Wingate got Sari assigned to him. She gon' come in here fussin', but she goin' to Dr. Wingate's."

"Good, and I been working on the wagon at Doc's place. He been good to us, Junie. I pray dis don't hurt him and Deliah none. Neva seen a white man love a Negra like he love Deliah."

"Papa, do you think that people don't know?"

"Dey know, son. Dats de way of dis world. But one day, we gon' be free. They talkin' 'bout it now. Everywhere I's go, white folk riled, say Lincoln gon' try to make us free. We gots to go. It gon' get worse for it get betta."

"Papa, Colorado gon' be good. This here horse trainer said, 'James Beckworth, a real live colored mountain man!' Oooh wee, Papa. I'm so glad the voice said go west."

"Sho' hope he right, 'cause Canada make more sense to me."

John got up, opened Junie's coat, and they took out the supplies he brought and added them to their hidden cache of items under the lined spot they dug in the dirt, under the table.

"Might have to eat some of this on da morrow. Ol' Rubin say I gots to be there early and scrub de stairs for running down 'em. Massa say no food for two days."

Slapping his hands hard together, John gritted his teeth. "Man wanna protect what's his. I's gon' fix this wagon like you heard, Junie like Noah built the ark and it gon' fly across the land. By da time dey recognize we gone, we be too far to catch."

Junie walked over and hugged his father fiercely. John clutched him to his stomach.

They would be gone, or they would be dead. There was no other choice.

Chapter Four

1859

The place was so busy when they got up the next morning that everyone was moving fast, running here and there, and frantic to get it all done. The Massa determined during the night that he wanted Christmas within the next three days because he had never not had Christmas with the Missus, and since she was not going with him for the holiday, he would have two. One with her and one with his sons and family later. He also decided to make it a merry event and invite his neighbors.

So, they worked until weary to the bone in order for Massa Benson could have two Christmases when they, as slaves, never really had one. It was Sari's last day before she went to Dr. Wingate's, and Missus had the bright idea that the workers would have their Christmas on the regular Christmas Day. This way, they could all be on hand to work and make sure her early Christmas Day festivities were the event of the season with all the other planters.

Junie was tired. So tired that his gumption had got to talking to his get up and go and was gone. He looked at his sister, Sari, who had gotten away for a bit after helping in the kitchen for the big house that night. Massa Benson had a heap of folk laughing and eating and carrying on 'cause it be Christ Jesus early birthday party. He reckoned that them folk loved to put on airs and such, and his birthday was a good reason to kick up their heels. He loved him some actual baby Jesus day, 'cause it allowed

27

them to all be together. But this practice run was good too. Sari never had to fetch and carry for Missus when outside neighboring women folk came to the big house. She was kept in the kitchen. Massa Benson was particular that way. Cinda once said, "Some folk didn't mind sinning in the dark, long as no light exposed it and all." Junie didn't understand her remark, but it rang true because when they came in, Sari left out.

He sighed. "I'se plum tired, Papa. Got this feeling way down in c'here that I'se going to always be tired."

Junie rested his hand on his chest as he moved around the shack. They could all hear old Rufus fiddle sweetly, churning out music fit for royalty. Most folk in the quarters had left the circle because they were just as tired. They had ate as Massa Benson wanted them to so his neighbors could see how he treated them so good with good food and all. He even had them line up to receive their one item of clothing. You could have pants, shirt, or dress, skirt. You couldn't have both. Massa Benson was never ever real generous; just enough to give the appearance of good.

Junie had heard his papa say some folk got their satisfaction from what a thang look to be, not what it was.

Shoulders slumped, Junie sighed louder.

Sari peeked at her little brother and wondered at his unusual morose mood. Junie's daily sunny attitude could put a body off if one didn't know that Junie spent most of his days in his head, thinkin' up thangs that usually made Massa plenty of money for the Benson Plantation. They had three hundred twenty-three slaves working from sunup to sundown. The fields might be backbreaking, but it was at the big house where a soul couldn't rest. Missus calling Sari and needing her all the time. She needed her brow dapped, her bottom wiped, then the bucket removed. Some nights, she got her up just to scratch an itch Missus coulda reached herself. This was supposed to be the one day a year she had to herself. Now, she had to go see about Dr. Wingate and his place.

Jesus wasn't the only who wept.

John Benson ran through it all in his head again. He couldn't mess up. They was gon' run. He ran his hands and skimmed over the twine his beloved had braided into a bracelet for him. She always knew more than most. She talked to the good Lord Jesus all the time and foretold many thangs. Her loss was still a hole in his stomach he had never been able to fill. How can you move forward when the best part of you was in the past? He loved his children, but nothing in dis world made you believe that you could keep love. He'd never known love to be kind. It was like Massa in that way. You can have a shirt, no pants. He could have their love in the past but not the future.

He fingered the twine on his wrist. "You told me what to do, beloved, and now's the time to do it. I promised he'd never get his hands on our Sari, and I'm gon' keep that promise."

Later in the evening, Junie spoke to his father as they readied to bed down for the night. "It's hard work, Papa, having the smarts but always playin' dumb. Ya reckon dey miss da part dat if I can figure out how to water dem plants with less labor, I can figure out how to read?"

John thought awhile and then took his time answering. Having a son as bright as Junie encouraged him to be slow to respond, so he answered right. "Small power always like to believe it's bigger than it is, until its tiny spark meets a flame. Just keep hidin' ya flame. Long as dey feel all powerful, dey don't ever believe we can live beyond dey puppet strings. Dem letters you read say when they auctioning off Sari?"

"Nah, suh. Just New Year. But voice say be gon' by Christmas. Her being at Dr. Wingate gon' put her out of da way."

"It gon' be close, but it sho' gon' git done. Pure blessin' Massa be gone." Twizzling the straw in his mouth, John rubbed his stomach. "That was good eatin' at the circle."

"Yes'm, it was. You thinking that Sari gon' know how to cook now?"

"Cinda been teaching her every day. She don't know why; just think Cinda don' got mad at her for some reason. Cinda got love for all of us."

Choosing not to say who Junie felt Cinda had love for, he asked, "Can we practice kickin' and knockin'?"

John smiled. "Sho' we will. You be a fighta before long."

Junie knew that Cinda had to teach Sari how to cook with the idea that one day she'd have to take care of the household she'd run. But Cinda knows they are leaving so her assignment from his papa is to teach her good campfire food.

Lord, teach her good, so her food don't choke us dead.

Chapter Five

Present

Nodding his head, Zachary looked at his five best men. They were as ready as they could get with the scarcity of information they were given. They had excellent questions, and he had zero answers. He could only tell them that they were all good men and whatever they needed to do, they would because they were built that way. They understood improvisation. He had brought them all in from his days in the army. Not all were ex-Special Forces, but they were extraordinary men. Determined, loyal, and of strong character. They were Zachary's chosen. He dismissed them and sat and waited.

The wait was short. William Thornton, better known as Bebop because he always heard music in his head and bounced to the beat, was his one ex-Special Forces employee and his current best friend. It got so that the team would look at Bebop while on special missions to see if his head was bopping. A bopping head was an all-clear. A still head meant something was off. It was unfortunate that the day his head was still, no one was in range to see it but him. The insurgents had jammed communication, but they had all been there before and survived. They were determined that this time would not be different. Although the enemy had Bebop pinned down in a kill box, they didn't know he was down ammo and had taken a bullet to his upper thigh. The realization that one of theirs was trapped made them all go commando. They took chances that they were all known to vote down in the past, but this was Bebop, and nothing would stop them from seeing that big, round, chocolate face and those huge dimples dance around the barracks just one more time. He was family; they all were.

When they finally cut through to him, he had taken another bullet to the shoulder but was valiantly fighting on. The team covering them, Zachary grabbed Bebop and ran in a zigzag formation to their assigned pickup point. Popping smoke, they waited, battling it out until the helicopter came and provided ground cover as they ascended and were out. Two months later, Bebop was released from the rehabilitation center and the army.

Bebop had struggled for a while as husband, father, and provider. His letters were full of feeling that civilian life was not for him, but he had no entry back to what he knew. Then Zachary had gotten out and obtained his position at Burstein Labs, head of security. Bebop, with his limp, was his first hire. He wanted to make him second in command, but that choice was taken out of his hands. Still, the man who was the best man at his wedding, who was godfather to his son, was his *real* second in command. As such, he knew to leave with the others, then circle around and return for the real briefing.

Walking in with his head bobbing, Bebop asked, "Are we actually going to see some action?"

"That's what I'm hearing, but what kind of action is the question," Zachary said, his fingers meeting in a point under his chin as he strategized several possible best moves in his head.

"I can see the old noggin ticking, so tell me how we going to play this out," Bebop said, as he flipped a chair around and straddled it as he sat.

"They know you're ex-Special Forces but don't know you're my best friend. Just like I thought, keeping it chill between us at work has been an advantage. Not even Sylvia knows you work here. I'm going to place you close to whatever is coming. You'll be my eyes and ears."

"I got your six. Always and forever. You plan to Barney style this plan to Tom?"

Zachary sucked his teeth. "Uh, no! Bringing that knuckle dragger into any plan is a plan to fail. I once told him, 'As you were,' and the fool went home. Nah, man, we good right here. You recon and report only to me." Zachary arched his eyebrow in response and waited.

Shrugging, Bebop said, "I'd like to think that this is not where I came to . . . to die of boredom, not after all the action we saw."

"Well, I have a feeling we are finally about to see what really happens in this place. Let's hope we don't both regret ever coming here."

Rising, Bebop asked the question hanging in the air whenever they were together. "Had enough yet?"

Zachary balled up a piece of paper off his desk and threw it at him. "That will be all, William."

"Did you just use my government name when it's just the two of us together? Now, I know I've overstayed my welcome. I'll be here with the rest of the team when you signal."

Zachary shook his head. Bebop always asked him if he "had enough" to test the temperature of his marriage. He wanted to tell him so many times, "Yes, I've had enough." But the army had forged him strong, and he couldn't—wouldn't—throw in the white towel yet and admit defeat.

Zachary thought about his failing marriage and thought he'd make the effort. Pulling out his cell, he called Sylvia. "Hey, babe. I'm probably going to be late coming home tonight. There may be some overtime involved."

"Well, thanks for telling me so late, Zachary. I've already ordered you a meal, which was delivered a little while ago. I'll just put it in the microwave for you. I was going to go out for a while, but my event got canceled. So I guess I'll be here when you get home," Sylvia said, her tone lifeless and lacking any enthusiasm to see him.

Hesitating in his response, Zachary wanted to ask her if ordering a meal she didn't cook or pay for was such a strain on her day. And she knew his regular hours to get off were two hours away, so why was she ordering him food so early? Can't a man get a *hot* meal? A little consideration? They had someone come in every week to do the housekeeping. She was rarely home, preferring her girlfriends to staying in. Once a week on Tuesday, like clockwork, she rolled over and provided her wifely duties sans kiss. She usually had a look of total disdain if he cared to look at her while she performed the laziest sex he had ever had the misfortune of engaging in.

He heard the echo of, "Had enough yet?" Shaking the voice free from his head, he answered Sylvia, "Yes, I'll see you then, if you're not already asleep."

"Yes, well, it isn't Tuesday. And the one thing I am sure of is that when things are so very boring around here, there's always sleep."

Zachary didn't need to respond because she had already hung up. He wasn't sure what the future held at his job or in his home, but he had to believe that he deserved better than this. Didn't everyone?

As he leaned back in his chair, his mind was boggled about decisions he knew he would have to make. His ears picked up on static transmissions coming from his computer's main dashboard. He swiveled around and looked at the numerous monitors. Each represented different areas of the building and outside grounds. Standing, he peered at leaves floating aboveground on Monitor C and treetops swaying adjacent on Monitor D. Checking out a hunch, he panned one camera around to the deserted heliport. This area hadn't even been identified on camera or monitor because he was advised it was not relevant to his job. Calling Bebop in late at night, he had him reprogram the camera and computer to pick up this area too. He didn't buy the company line even then and followed his instinct to cover his butt.

Dust was swirling. Landing was an MH-X Stealth Black Hawk helicopter, the type that was hard to pick up on any radar . . . the type that was used to get Bin Laden in 2011. The kind that people were still not supposed to know about, at least not nonmilitary personnel. A tingling slithered down his spine.

"What in the 'I'm gon' have to kill something before this thing is over' is going on?"

Why did Burstein Lab have this type of equipment? Why did he have no knowledge that they owned this type of equipment? He knew there was a heliport, but many buildings had amenities left from previous owners that were never used.

As they landed and before anyone came out of the helicopter, several men in white lab coats ran out of a door with gurneys.

As Zachary stared at a cell phone and desk phone that failed to ring, he called on his men. He didn't know what was going on, but they would be willing and able, even if Burstein Labs didn't want them to be.

After all, that's what he was paid for, and he planned for once to earn his keep.

Zachary fell asleep in his office, waiting on the phone call that didn't come. He was disturbed in more ways than one. Disturbed by the fact that Edgar Burstein still had not called him about whatever was going on at Burstein Labs and disturbed because his recurring dreams from years before were back. This one was so real that Zachary felt it in the very heart of his being. It stirred him still. It was a precious feeling. He would hold on and savor its memory as long as he could.

Zachary stood behind a door. Hesitating to enter, he pushed it open and peeked inside. Although it was night and the room was dark, he could see a silhouette. There lay a body, slender but womanly in all her curves. He approached silently, willing her to turn around, knowing that green eyes would be his undoing if they opened to him, only him. He breathed in deeply and smelled . . . woman. In anticipation, he shut his eyes to relish the aroma and pull it close to him. As he opened his eyes, she stood face-to-face with him. But it was dark, and the only shine in the room illuminated cascading ripples of hair and large, jade-green eyes. Supple arms came up and caressed him around his broad shoulders, lips that he had waited to kiss since his early teen years enveloped his in soft, pillowing bliss. He pulled her to him, and they fit, key to lock. Her breathing caught, and his echoed the same rhythm.

She was home.

Chapter Six

1859

"We got some good eatin' today, Papa. Merry Christmas!" Junie said as he went through the stack of food and blankets they had accumulated over the last two months.

"Yeah, we gon' make our way to freedom later tonight. 'Member to put no liquor in my cup when ya brin' it. And don't cha—"

"—Papa, I got dis. It gon' be all right. The voice say, we gon' leave dis place in peace. Massa gave us his three days of no work, like every year. One day already gone, today we leave, one mo' day befor' we missed."

Sari was still at Dr. Wingate's small farm. She was angry with everyone for missing the festivities. Usually, those slaves working on other plantations are allowed to get a pass and come home for the holidays, but they had made sure Dr. Wingate had told her no.

Papa laughed quietly. "Right 'bout now, yo' sistah causing Dr. Wingate all kinda trouble."

"She spoiled, Papa. Don't even know she bein' fattened for the auction block. It ain't gon' be pleasant riding with her thinkin' she leavin' her home."

"Nah, ya right. But may hap some ground under way, help her see betta. We know we doin' what's best. Can't fly when you tied to a mountain. Massa been a mountain of hurt and pain all our lives. I just wish I coulda did betta when yo' mama was c'here."

Junie came over and hugged his father around the waist. The affection between them was genuine and constant. In a world where you were motherless and chattel, somebody had to spoon-feed you love, or the brittleness of this life would break you.

"Papa, she be free now. Freer than any of us. And, I 'member old preacher saying, if you speak to the mountain, it'd be moved. Massa gon' hear us loud and clear."

Giving a decisive nod, John put on his coat and left the cabin. Junie looked after him in the early-morning glow and saw Cinda meet him by the smithy. She grabbed his arm, and together, they disappeared around the back. He was sad that Cinda couldn't run with them, but the voice didn't name her, and she was such an intricate part of the daily functions of the big house that taking her would be suicide. So Junie prayed all would be well for her and his papa's time together. Junie understood some goodbyes had to be private.

Junie wrapped everything back up and placed the bundles in sacks. Then when it was time to leave, they would only have to grab and go. Putting on his coat, he looked around the room and knew he wouldn't sleep one more night in the prison he was forced to call home.

"Almost there, Mama," he whispered.

The plantation was alive, and everyone was headed to the big house. It gleamed with tallow candles already lit and a huge Christmas tree in the window. The slaves gathered in front of the massive porch that held stone figurines on both sides of the porch steps. In the summer, they would explode with colors as the flowers reached high in the sky. Even now, the holly and greenery draping the railings bespoke wealth and holiday cheer. The children were exuberant in their play as they waited for their candy, and maybe they would be able to grab a penny or two when it was thrown out into the yard. They would also receive hand-me-down toys that they awaited each year. The adults were waiting for their package of clothing and the enormous amount of food and alcohol that would flow freely. Most got drunk and slept away the next day, nursing a hangover.

Junie stood on his tiptoes, looking for his father. He soon saw him come around the corner, holding on to Cinda's arm, giving her a slight squeeze as she went through the back to help serve the food she had spent the last three days cooking. When Junie asked her if she minded having to work on a day others were free, she replied, "No, chile. It's my Christmas present to everyone. Dis be the best I cook all year, 'cause it's from my heart."

Junie was glad to hear that because he wanted to enjoy the ham, turkey, and rabbits with all the fixings. And the desserts would be something he couldn't even think about, or he'd have to start there.

Old Rubin began to ring the bell as the house servants, and the rest of the plantation came to join those already outside. Missus slowly walked out the door with a handkerchief over her nose and mouth and muffled her speech.

"Gather 'round; don't dawdle. Master Benson is not here today, and it is on me to do this year's festivities. As I am unwell, you will be allowed to come into the home in an orderly fashion, eat and drink—"

She was interrupted by the cheering.

"My goodness, you people can at least have the good manners to allow me to finish. Oh, what am I saying? You don't know any better." Then with a catch in her throat, she motioned for Rubin to bring the large box forward.

Opening the box, she called from behind its lid, "Line up, youngest first and get your Christmas present."

The children were positioned based on size and came forward to get their Christmas gifts. As they accepted the gift, each child said very nicely, "Thank ya, Missus. Merry Christmas."

Each parent smiled and nodded as their child went through. Junie, knowing the missus didn't like him, did exactly like the others and got out of the way after getting his gift. He peeled the newspaper open, gently folded it again, and placed the paper in his coat pocket. Paint was chipping off the wooden soldier he had received. He noticed little Ron had also received a soldier. He would give his soldier to him before he left so his soldier would have someone to fight.

Snapping back to attention, he looked to the side and saw Cinda motioning for him to enter through the back door. If Cinda could cook, he guessed his Christmas gift would be to serve everyone one last time.

Walking off, Junie waved quickly to his father as he saw him accept his clothing package for his Christmas gift.

Sauntering into the kitchen, the first person Junie spied was Gussie. "Well, now, Junie. Ya mighty chipper for a boy who got to work when others is playin'. Don't 'member ya bein' so happy to work befo'."

"Leave the young'n alone, Gussie. You worry 'bout getting the rest of these here fixings on dat table. Folk been waitin' all year for dis meal. So let's mak'em smile."

"All right, Cinda. I know how ya sweet on dat John, and Junie ain't gon' neva do wrong in yo' eyes."

Cinda looked at Junie with a sheen of sadness in her gaze. "Ya right 'bout dat, Gussie. Junie always gon' be in my heart. Always."

Junie turned from both women and wiped the tear threatening to run down his face. He had studied hard not to lose it in front of Cinda. She was the only thang he regretted. Leaving her was leaving a part of his heart. She had been what he thought a mother would be, and he loved her.

Cinda smiled his way and lifted her head to the sky as though telling him it would be okay. "Grab dat ham platter and take it out dere, den come back fot de rest. Let's make dis meal as dough it's de last one."

Gussie snorted. "I don't want to thank of nothin' as my last one. I want to be c'here 'morrow and the next day. You'se talkin' pure de nonsense, Cinda. Uh, uh, uh."

Junie grabbed the platter and took it to the table. He returned with Gussie and Cinda five more times before it was all laid out.

Rubin then spoke after the last item, the bread, was placed. "We gon' take this time to thank the Massa and Missus for a wonderful meal. Dey didn't have to, but dey good peoples to us, who don't deserve it. I will pray for y'all ungrateful souls now . . ."

Junie wanted to giggle when he heard Ol' Silas whisper to his papa, "Dat man don't know nothin'. Massa break wind, and he say, 'cuse me."

John laughed as he stuffed his mouth and ate. Junie could tell his father was thinking of the journey before them and the miles they would need to cover.

God-willing, Colorado was just one month of hard travel in front of them. A four-horse team, extra springs incorporated in the wagon design, food, supplies . . . They would make it.

When the alcohol started flowing, Rubin was right there urging folk to drink up. Junie tried to be there to fill his father's cup, but he sometimes didn't beat Rubin to the refill. It almost felt like Rubin knew something. Junie was concerned but told himself if his father did have to drink the alcohol, it wasn't much.

When the people began to get rowdy with all the liquor they had abided, Rubin escorted them out of the room and into the yard leading to the slave quarters. In times past, they would have music and dancing in the house, but with Jacob Benson gone, Missus decided they could eat, drink, and leave. As they went outside, music began to play.

The fiddle and drums called out to all that it was their time now. Soon, the people would play a game called "John Kunering." The John Kunering consisted of the men dressed in rags and animal skins, playing homemade instruments, singing, dancing, and marching from cabin to cabin to perform for Massa and overseer. Those who witnessed the show were to reward the men with money and alcohol. In the past, Jacob Benson and his guests would stand and watch and then give the players more alcohol and some coin to act the fool. Rubin took the place of Jacob Benson this year with overseers in place to make sure no one thought to wander off. Rubin was plenty with the alcohol and short on the coin. Some husbands and wives, who reunited from different plantations, went into their cabins early, swaying to the beats of their homeland that encompassed the quarters.

It was a different celebration with Jacob Benson away. Junie saw the overseers taking several nips of the alcohol as the people danced and cheered. Junie ran and eagerly made sure their cups never ran dry. However, Rubin was a problem. He didn't drink, and he didn't blink. He just kept his eye on everyone.

Junie felt someone fall over on him, singing and smelling of booze. He turned, astounded to find out it was his father. "Papa? Papa?"

"Ugggh," he stumbled. "Dance, Junie boy. Urggh . . ." John sang in a gravelly voice, his words slurred, alcohol reeking. He would take a step, and then he would stop and burp as he weighed Junie down with his ox-strong arms.

Rubin walked over and stared at his father in derision. "Dis Negra c'here ain't nothin'."

Junie fisted his hands. It would feel good to kick Ol' Rubin for treating his papa so badly.

John's half eyelids peeked at Rubin and crowed, "'Cuse me, Rubin." Then he laughed aloud at the earlier joke Old Silas had made about Rubin. "'Cuse me, Massa!"

John then fell on the seat of his pants and hit the ground laughing. "Ya sometin', Rubin. Ya stand dere mighty as an old oak. Ya watch when de rains come. Ya don't get struck by de lightening so far in the clouds your head tips."

Rubin bent down to John's level. "What ya know 'bout me, boy? What ya know 'bout my pain?" Rubin then dusted off his thighs as he rose. "Foolish talk from a Negra in de dirt where he belong."

Junie watched the back-and-forth in awe. He'd never seen his father go toe-to-toe with Rubin before. He must be very drunk, and what would that mean for them? Then when his father crawled around the ground to get up, Junie felt freedom slipping through his hands.

Swallowing his thoughts, Junie asked, "Can ya help me get him to our cabin?"

Rubin looked down at Junie and gave a loud, full-belly laugh. "Negra, please!"

He walked away and said something to Ol' Silas as he passed him. Ol' Silas quickly came over to Junie, and without saying a word, he bent down, placed his father's arm around his neck, and helped Junie get him home.

As he was leaving, Ol' Silas scratched his head and looked over his shoulder as he grabbed the door. "In all my time with ya papa, neva seen him drunk. Be well, boy." Then he slammed the door.

John then sat up. "Ya okay dere, son?"

Junie turned with a smile opening across his face. "Ya not drunk, Papa?"

"No, boy. We got thangs to do. But Rubin was eagle eye'd dis c'here day. So I splashed some alcohol on my clothes and played de fool."

"Dat was smart, Papa."

"Yeah, well, ya had to get it from somebody. Guess it was me."

Junie smiled and joked, "Oh, I thought it was Mama."

John moved the table for Junie to grab all the sacks he had prepared. He then gathered all their bedding up but left a thin layer on the straw pallets. He didn't want them to know he was gone if they checked. Dr. Wingate had the pot and skillet they would take and even the outside fire pit they would need to cook each night. But the first night, they would only eat what Cinda had packed for them.

When John showed Junie half a ham, cheese, corn bread, and cake, Junie's eyes lit up. He hadn't eaten well, being too excited and scared to be hungry.

"Doc got lots of jugs of water already on de wagon. We gon' walk de mares out of the pen, real quiet like, like we practiced. When we get far enough out, we gon' ride hard. We just need to wait until all is quiet, and we gon' make our way. Get ya what sleep you can, son."

Junie bobbed his head and sat at the table. He lay his head down and waited for his father to tap him, telling him it was time.

When the tap came, Junie was disoriented. He didn't understand what he saw. Colorado couldn't have gleaming steel carriages rolling down cemented roads. Why did the big square box have color and moving pictures in it? Then the voice called out so gently. "*Later.*"

John called Junie's name loud, as though he had been calling him more than once. "Junie, I's talkin' to you. Get moving, and don't cha stop for nothin'."

"I promise not to stop for nobody, Papa."

Together, they tiptoed silently around the land of their birth. They knew every rock, every groove in the frozen grass as they approached the corral, where the horses neighed. But John Benson, Horse Whisperer, had them quiet in no time. He pulled out the two they had chosen, and without saddles, they walked them around the perimeter of the plantation. They stayed away from the main roads and stuck to the patch of trees where they couldn't be seen, even if someone was looking for them. Finally, when they got to the part of the trees and roads making a fork that his father had told him about, his father whispered one fevered word.

"Ride."

Galloping for all they were worth, John and Junie flew across the land. It would take thirty minutes to ride to Dr. Wingate's and another thirty minutes to get Sari in the wagon. Everything had to be precise to pull this off. John looked back over his shoulder at Junie, and the look on John's face pleaded for Junie to keep up. Sweating, his inner thighs burning, Junie hit his feet against the hind parts of his horse and flew past his father.

"Dats it, Junie, fly!"

Junie grinned until his teeth hurt. So this was what it was like—this was *free*.

Chapter Seven

1859

Slowing down, John motioned for Junie to get off his horse and begin walking again. As they approached the farm, they stood behind trees and watched it for a stretch of time before they went around to the back. This was a doctor's farm, and John knew people could show up with any kind of mishap or illness, day or night. He and the doctor had discussed it, and there was a place they could hide if that happened. It was Sari they had to worry about in that instance.

Knocking on the back door, Delia answered and motioned as John and Junie came through the door. "Mighty thanks to ya, Ms. Delia."

"It's not a problem, John. And this must be Junie. What a handsome young man you are. Doctor Wingate already said you were smart."

Junie's heart fluttered, his hands sweated, and his mouth fell open. She was a vision. She was so beautiful that he wanted to touch her to see if she was real. Her thick hair was tight with natural curls and bounced as she glided across the floor. When she bent to light the lanterns, her curvy figure drew his twelve-year-old eyes to territory he had never dared to look at before. His heart beat so fast that he wanted to ask his father if he was having a heart attack. He turned around, only to see his father looking at him with a snicker on his face.

"You'se be all right," he whispered.

Doctor Wingate then coughed, and they both looked up and saw him leaning against the doorway. "Delia, dear, I see you have met our young genius."

"Yes, I have. You didn't tell me how handsome he was, Doctor."

"Ahh, that's because I didn't want him to steal your heart."

Doctor Wingate and Delia stared at each other with a secret communication between them.

Delia then turned and said, "No chance of that happening, although he is a might tempting." Grabbing the tail of her dress, she moved toward the door. "I'll get Sari. Then finally, I can stop playing sick."

When she left the room, Junie exclaimed, "How come she talk like you, Doctor Wingate?"

Dr. Wingate's eyes lifted, and his lips grinned as though a fond memory was just at the tip of his fingers. "She wanted to talk that way, Junie. I was fine with her the way she was, but she wanted to learn, and being a very smart woman, she did. She can read too."

Shaking his head, Junie mumbled, his cheeks still scarlet, "I just ain't neva seen such a thang."

"Papa? Junie? Is sometin' wrong?" Sari asked as she flew into the room.

"Nah, Sari girl, everythan' right. We runnin', and we leavin' now," John said in a no-nonsense tone.

Sari tilted as though she would faint. Delia brought smelling salts out of her pocket and waved it under Sari's nose.

John and Junie looked askance at Delia. "We've already had a number of fits while she was here. A fit about being here. A fit about not going home for Christmas. A fit about having to serve her own Christmas dinner for the first time."

John hung his head in shame. "Sari girl, I love ya. But ya got to stop try'n to be like de missus. She ain't nobody ya should be lookin' up to da way ya do. Now, tell Ms. Delia ya sorry, girl."

Rolling her eyes, Sari stomped her foot and stayed silent.

Junie looked at his sister with sadness. "How come ya always on da other side of da road, Sari? If me and Papa say red, ya say blue. We don't have time for dis. I want to be free if ya don't!"

Sari advanced toward her brother with her hand stretched out. He knew he had never spoken to her in such a way before, but he was plum tired of her acting as though she were a member of the massa's household when she was just like them.

"Ya don't want me to go, Junie?" Sari asked quietly.

Looking her straight on, he said in an adult voice, "Not if ya gon' act like ya acting. We don't need it. We goin' to Colorado to be free. Been plannin' it for a long time, but we couldn't tell ya, 'cause de way ya see thangs be contrary. Ya think ya good, and ya just a pet like Lucy, Missus little dog."

"I ain't no dog, Junie!"

John looked out the window, "Daybreak in 'bout an hour. We gots to go. Yea or nay, Sari girl? You'se grown. If it's no, it'll break my heart. Ya mama would tell ya to run and run fast. Bad days is comin', Sari. Massa just waitin' to give ya to the man wit' de most coin in his pocket."

"Missus would neva—"

"No! Ya not gon' tell me what Missus not gon' do. She gon' do what Massa say. He in charge of dat house. He neva gon' let Missus tell him what to do 'bout his money."

Sari gulped. "But . . . but—"

Rubbing his large hand over his tight curls, John sighed. "Do what I ax of ya. Stay c'here until it's time fa' de doctor to take ya back. Den act like ya didn't know we was gon'. Keep Dr. Wingate and his bizness out ya mouth. I love ya, gal."

John grabbed Sari and hugged her hard. Junie then did the same.

Sari slumped into a chair and cried into her hands. When she stood up, John and Junie had already quietly gone out the door to the barn with the doctor.

Junie's shoulders sagged, and he walked reluctantly behind his father.

"Her choice; dis her life, Junie."

"Neva thought she'd pick dem, Papa."

"She not picking dem, son; she pickin' easy."

Uncovering the wagon, they began to unpack what they had stored on each horse unto the wagon, with the two horses already hitched to it.

Junie stooped down and looked under the carriage, and it looked just like he had told his father to make it. "She run good, Papa?"

"Like the wind!"

"Papa, two mo' horses gon' be waitin' for us down de road?"

"We stick to de plan. Doc c'here got some waitin' on us, but I gots to look like bizness as always. Can't be seen wit' four when two will do. Dese walking horses is what dey use to seeing. We don't change what folk use to seeing; den dey don't see us at all."

As they packed, they heard hoofbeats clamoring up to the front of the house. Doctor Wingate put his hand out and cautioned them to be quiet. He then went out of the barn, closing the door behind him. Before John could say a word, Junie had hightailed it out the door to the back of the house and crept along the ground behind a bush on the side of the porch to listen.

"Delia, girl, go fetch your massa. Last night, my oldest boy had too much to drink and fell off the top-floor landing. I need Doc to come quick."

"Yes, suh, Mister Plessy. I's gon' get him now," she said.

Junie wanted to laugh. She sounded just like them, and the man was none the wiser. He heard Dr. Wingate at the front porch as he crawled closer and listened from the side. "Too much merrymaking, huh? I'll be right there, directly. Let me get my horse and bag. You go on back and ask them to have some hot water boiled and make sure he doesn't go to sleep."

"Thanks, Doc. I'll go now."

The man jumped on his horse and hightailed it out of there. Junie stood and walked to the back of the house until the horse and rider were out of sight.

"You making a habit of listening at doors, Junie?"

"'Spect I do wat's needed, Dr. Wingate, suh. It's just bein' young and a Negra sometimes you'se got to find truth any way ya can."

Grabbing his medical bag, the doctor walked with Junie back to the barn. There was still no sign of Sari, which made Junie want to cry, but she had to make her own decision. But he also knew the voice said she was to go too. So maybe he should tell her that.

When the doctor headed for the barn, Junie turned and headed back to the house. He found Sari still sitting where he left her, crying her eyes out.

"Sari girl," he said, as he placed his arms around her and softly whispered into her ears, "the voice said we all must go, Sari. Me, ya, and Papa."

Sari wiped her eyes on her apron. "Truly, Junie?"

"Yes, Sari, truly."

She rose to pack, covering her face with her apron, when Delia came into the room with her sack already packed.

"Here you go, baby. Your papa and brother want you to be free." She then placed her hand on her stomach. "Being free to be themselves is the best gift a parent can give their child. Merry Christmas, Sari."

Biting her lip, Sari grabbed the sack and then hugged Delia. "Thanks, and I'm sorry 'bout acting out."

Delia floated to the door and ushered them out. When Junie passed her, she bent over and kissed him on his cheek. Then holding his cheek and smiling like a jack-o'-lantern, Junie ran to the barn. When he opened the door, Sari ran past him to her father.

"I's sorry, Papa. I tol' Delia I's sorry too."

Dr. Wingate secured his medical bag to the saddle and mounted his horse. "I usually take my wagon, but since I didn't leave immediately, this will help me make up the time. This man makes clumsy a habit. This is his third accident this year. It's been a pleasure knowing all of you. I truly believe no man should own another. Godspeed. Please let me know you made it." He then reached out and gave John a slip of paper.

John handed the paper to Junie, and Junie read it. "Ya movin' to New York?"

"For a season. Delia's with child. We were willing to play this game while it was just the two of us. But a child spells a different type of problem. She or he will be born free."

"Congratulations, Doc," John said, going over to him on the horse and shaking his hand.

"Thank you. We'll stay in New York until the baby's birth, and then we're moving to Canada. And, John, please call me Donald at least once before we leave each other's company."

"I can do dat. Thank you . . . Donald."

Dr. Wingate raised his hat in farewell and galloped out like the hounds of hell were nipping at his heels.

Perhaps they are, Junie thought.

Junie jumped up into the wagon, and Sari got on beside him. His father sat there and looked up.

"Lord, we axing for ya to be our eyes. We axing for ya to be our ears. Place us in yo' loving arms. We thank ya now for freedom. Keep Cinda, Dr. Wingate, I means, Donald, and Delia. Amen."

Junie and Sari chorused, "Amen."

Sari fell asleep almost before they were good down the rugged dirt road. Junie nudged her. "Dey worked you dat hard, Sari girl?"

"No, I'se been havin' trouble sleepin'. I keep hearin' Mama talkin' to me. Some things she told me to do 'fa she died and to neva stop doin'. In my dreams, she's tellin' me to relax now." Sari hesitated, leaned forward, and whispered, "Den dere's dis man—"

Junie put up his finger, then surreptitiously eased up to look over his shoulder to the wagon seat, making sure his father continued to drive the horses and could not hear them speaking. Then, lying back down on the pallets in the back, he hurriedly spilled, "Hush, gal, ya don't know nothin' 'bout no man."

"Boy, I'se twenty to your'n twelve, so you don't shush me. I can see what was for me to talk to wit' a friend ain't meant for a knobby-headed little boy."

Contrite, Junie tried to dial back his angst. "Aww, gal, I'se just messin' wit' ya. What man?"

Rushing forward, Sari stammered. "He keep comin' in my dreams. I falls asleep, dere he come. It be so real, Junie. And this time, Junie, I kissed him!"

"Don't 'cha be lettin' no man kiss ya, Sari." Junie whispered furiously.

"Listen with *both* your'n ears, Junie. *I* kissed *him*." Sari placed her hands on her lips in wonder. "It was glorious, Junie. I ain't never been kissed afore."

"Ya still ain't, Sari. It was a dream, you ninny."

"Better than my real life, Junie."

Pretending he was tired, Junie turned over away from his sister and her dreams.

I'se just twelve, Lord. I ain't ready for all dis.

Chapter Eight

1860

The days had been hard, but their preparation had been thorough. They had been on the road a week. It had been Junie's idea to take four horses, reinforce the wagon, and carry three bricks to heat the fire for warmth. They had counted on everything except how inept Sari was in acclimating to life on the run.

"Papa, can we stop soon? My bottom is sore, and I'se tired," Sari complained.

Junie sighed. "Sari girl, it's still daylight. What ya gon' slow us down for? We been out here six days and eva mile, ya yakkin' more—"

"—Ya ain't de boss of me, Junie. I'se the oldest, so ya hush ya mouth. I'se tired and—"

John slapped the reins on the horses, "If ya both don't hush, I'ma make ya walk a while. De horses could use de rest."

There was quiet in the wagon for the next several miles. John was an even-tempered man, but the bickering between Junie and Sari was making even him irritable.

Junie pulled out the map Dr. Wingate gave him. "Papa, Donald says c'here dat we should be getting to a water hole soon."

Slapping the reins again, John said, "First off, ya don't call him Donald. Ya gon' be respeckful, Junie, even when a grown folk ain't respeckful to ya.

Dr. Wingate was better to us den most. He also lettin' us be known dat eva white man ain't da enemy."

Sari then chimed in. "Dats right. Missus was not my enemy. She was good to me."

"Like a pet dog, she was good to ya," Junie murmured.

"I heard that, Junie! I'ma tell ya one more—"

John looked up to the sky and said in a tired voice, "—If ya can't keep a civil tongue, don't use it."

Quiet reigned in the wagon again, and they all enjoyed the crisp, clean air in peaceful silence. Sari rose a couple of times and rubbed her bottom. Junie climbed to the back and folded a blanket, and when he crawled back to the front, he motioned for Sari to sit on the blanket. She smiled and gave him a one-arm hug.

Rolling a piece of straw in his mouth, John said, "We gon' stop early today. When we make it to the watering hole, we gon' put up the wagon bows and then cover it with canvas. I think we far enough away now to make dis a covered wagon. We can soak some beans over a fire and add the last of the ham Cinda gave us to the mix. It's gon' be some stomach pleasin' eatin'. Junie, ya can add in pieces of de onion for mo' flavor. It's New Year's Day!"

Junie smiled in relief. His papa had known all along the miles they had traveled. He and Sari often had to lie in the back of the wagon under canvas as they traveled. Putting up the cover would have been a red flag to anyone used to seeing his papa on his way that something was unusual. Once the bows were out of the back and the canvas strung, there would be more room for Sari in the back. Maybe then she wouldn't complain so much.

"Papa, God been good dat no snow has met us, huh?" Sari asked.

"Ya, He has. I give thanks."

"Me too," Junie said. "Papa, ya missin' Cinda?"

"Sometin' fierce."

Junie twitched his mouth in thought. "Love hard, huh, Papa?"

"I 'spect so. But if ya not free to love and protect, it's dat harder."

"Protect, Papa?" Sari asked, turning her head to look at her father's forehead tighten at her question.

Nodding his head and slapping the reins hard, John pursed his mouth, then paused. Junie had noted that when his Papa slapped the reins, he was figuring hard—then John spoke his truth.

"When ya free, a man can say, 'Dats my chile; don't touch. My woman; don't touch.' When a man a slave, he swallow so much pain, love start to taste like acid, rollin' in ya stomach. Ya need to throw it up, but dat don't stop the taste in ya mouth. Each day, hot rage. So, ya learn to live in minutes."

Junie nodded understanding and sadness for his papa, but Sari didn't understand.

"Minutes, Papa? Why minutes? We got a whole wide world out c'here."

Sighing, John slapped those reins harder. "Sari, ya live in da minutes 'cause in da hour, or da days, one word from Massa and chile gon', wife gon'—or worse."

"Oh," Sari said in a tiny voice. "I'se sorry, Papa."

"Dats why we run, Sari. We run so dat we can live each day open to our own choices. Ya love who ya want to. Junie be who he want to be."

Junie then leaned forward. "Dere, Papa, da water."

John smiled, and Sari clapped. Then Junie said, "Papa, what say we leave the ham and beans for 'morrow and have us some fried fish today? We got some tatars too."

John beamed wide. "Dat sound good, Junie. Massa used to have me fish in da summer before I smithy, so I'se pretty good at it. And I brung a pole in the wagon. Dr. Wingate tol' me 'bout dem Colorado springs."

Pulling in between barren trees, John started giving directions. "Junie, tend to dese horses. They our best bet in stayin' ahead of whateva slave catchers Jacob Benson sent afta us. Den fill dem water jugs up. Sari, start us a fire. I's gon' start movin' de bows out the back of de wagon and get de canvas unfolded. When you finished with the jugs, Junie, come back c'here and hep me."

Everyone started bustling around. Junie ran to get his part done so they could put the cover over the wagon. He was tired of being cold and falling to the back of the wagon whenever someone was near, or they were near a town his papa was known in.

As the sun set and the cover was secured to the wagon, they all sat around the fire looking satisfied and well fed.

John looked at each of his children. "Dat was good eatin'. Bass was flowin' pretty good. Y'all full?"

"Ya, we are," Sari said, leaning back and looking up at the stars so bright.

"Papa!" Junie said, dropping his blanket and standing. "We in Illinois. We free, Papa!"

Laughing, John Benson stretched his arms over his head. "Junie, we was free de moment dis started. But ya right. Dr. Wingate say, we make it c'here, we can breathe easier."

Junie bent over and took a large gulp of Illinois rarified air. "Dis what freedom smell like, Papa." And Junie danced a jig on imagined music.

His imagination must have been powerful because Sari jumped and grabbed his arm and danced along. Soon, John joined, and they all joined hands in a circle and danced and shouted in laughter.

"Well, lookie here, Melvin. Darkies dancing in the night," the scraggly-looking white man said as his hardened face stared at the trio.

"I see 'em, brother. I also see food, a wagon, and the prettiest little darky gal I seen 'round these parts," his brother said, his pockmarked cheeks leering and licking his cracked lips.

John cursed and looked at Junie to motion him away from the fire. The more they spread out, the harder it would be to corral them together. John stared at them, and Junie knew his father was cataloging their strengths and weaknesses. How many times over the last months had his father taught him ways to defend himself and what to do if anything happened on the road? Separate, act scared and defenseless, and aim for the weakest part of a man. Don't stop fighting till they drop, and don't stay if they get the best of Papa. Keep Sari safe because she would be their weakness.

Junie stumbled farther backward, then fell on his knees with his hands up. "Please, suh, don't cha hurt us. We work hard fa' ya. Give ya what ya want," he cried.

"Don't hurt my daughta, Massa. We good, we good," John howled.

Sari's mouth fell open. She tried to run behind her papa, but he kept moving away.

"Brother, get the little darky tied up. I'll get the big one. They a sorry bunch, but we hit a payload."

The brother stalked toward Junie, and Junie saw the larger one dogged his father. They both reached their destinations at the same time. The man's stench almost whipped Junie good before he could put up his dukes. He gagged, staggered, and fell.

"Git up, you little butthole," the brother snarled and viciously reached down. As he grabbed . . . and caught a fistful of air . . . Junie scrambled back like a crab and kicked as hard as he could between the man's legs.

"Owww!" he bellowed as he crashed to his knees. When he went down, Junie popped up and kicked him as hard as he could in the chin, knocking him unconscious.

"What?" Melvin barked as he turned to see what had happened. He swiveled to assist his brother when John grabbed him from behind and placed his iron steel arm around his neck. He then braced his strength with his other arm and choked him until Melvin passed out.

"Ya good, Junie?" John yelled over as he took the rope meant for him and bound the ruffian.

"I'se fine, Papa," Junie said, falling back on his elbows in the dirt and breathing heavy.

Saying little, Sari walked over and took the rope off the fallen man Junie fought. Then holding her nose against the smell, she placed it in Junie's hand, motioning for him to get the villain tied up.

In a small voice, she murmured, "Thank ya, litt'l brotha."

Junie nodded as though his heart had not been beating outside of his chest. He rose, dusting himself off and feeling like a man. Then Junie mimicked his father's movements in tying up the man. He coughed a couple of times because rolling the man over released his stench. And he tried hard not to look into his face. He imagined him as any other animal that didn't want to go to slaughter. So he just trussed him up.

Walking over and yanking on the ropes Junie had used to secure his prisoner, John nodded his approval. "They probably won't have much, but let's get their horses unloaded and rubbed down. Check them for any money, and then pour out their saddlebags."

Pausing, John looked over at Sari. "Ya did good, gal. Don't cha put ya mind on what dey wanted to do. Put ya mind on dey couldn't do it. Me and Junie gon' protect you 'cause dat what men do, and I's proud to do it."

Sari ran over and threw her arms around her papa. Junie watched them and knew what his father was thinking. If it had been just days earlier, they wouldn't have been able to do anything but watch in impotent fury. Today, they took a measuring stick and could call themselves men. Over the years, as Sari got older, he saw how his papa distanced himself from her, as though waiting for something terrible to happen and bracing himself for the agony. He watched everybody making much over her looks, and with each, "She sho' is pretty," Papa's face grieved more. Junie finally understood what his innocent mind earlier did not.

Junie walked over and placed his arms around both of them. "Dis c'here runnin' thang da best thang eva. Huh, Papa?"

"Ya, son, it is," John said, disengaging from both of his children.

John strutted over and lifted each man and placed them far apart. He knew they would be waking up soon, and he wanted to get some sleep so that he would be on guard duty when they woke.

It was a restless night as the brother awoke and promised all types of retribution if his brother, Melvin, didn't wake up.

"You gon' leave me trussed up? I'm gon' kill ya, ya black monkey. I'm gon' strip ya back clean with a whip. I'm gon' rape ya daughter; then I'm gon' sell her to a whorehouse. I'm—"

"—I axed ya nicely to shut up, but okay," John said as he stuffed a folded bandana from their saddlebags into his mouth.

"Hey, what ya don' did dere, boy?! Ya better get that rag outta my brother's mouth. Ya hear me, you porch monkey?" Melvin shouted as he woke and wiggled around in a dazed way.

John lay down, not seeing any other material they could spare and not wanting to touch the odorous duo again. Junie closed his eyes too. He had helped his papa keep watch just in case, seeing as that's what men do.

Sari didn't awaken during the nighttime chaos. The dream was back, and she was knee-deep in the sin of it. The one where the man was so good-looking, he made a fuss in the center of her stomach. She saw him from time to time, more lately than ever. He called to her, but it was different than before. There was no stolen kiss because every time she reached out, something blocked his hand from hers. The barrier was gossamer-thin but did its job as though it were steel. As they stretched to touch, touching never came. Sari worried he was forbidden, and nothing could come from breaking through to the touch. It would be the end of life with Papa and Junie. And Papa and Junie were all she wanted to know.

Melvin continued to curse them until he wore himself to sleep. Then when he woke up, he started again as he saw each of them breaking camp to leave.

"Tie them horses to the back of the wagon, Junie. I checked dem over, and dey be all right. So, we take dem and give de other horses a spell of rest. We gon' move even faster dis way," John said as he reviewed what was in their saddlebags again.

Sari came from behind the trees, looking like a different person. Gone were the long, flowing tresses. Her thick, curly hair, kissed with the sun rays, was now in one braid down her back. Her homespun gown was under her arm as she strode forward in a pair of Junie's pants that fit her slim figure just right. Her green eyes sparkled with purpose, and she strolled into the camp with her chin high. One thing her dreams were telling her was that she was no longer a little girl, and as a free woman, she could make her own decisions.

"Papa, I took their blankets down to da water and did best I could to wash dem. Any critters sho''nuff should be gon'," Sari said as she moved around the campsite.

"Dats good, baby girl. Ya learnin'," John said and made no mention of her change in attire.

Sari beamed. Junie was proud of her. She didn't fall apart last night but got right up and did her part. But that didn't mean he wanted to share his few clothes with her.

Walking close to her, he mumbled, "Dat don' mean I'ma be wearing ya skirts, Sari girl."

"But ya gots such purty legs, Junie," Sari said with laughter.

John grunted when the raucous began again.

"Hey! Hey! You can't leave us like this. Bring your'n tar black ape tail over here and loose us," Melvin yelled.

"Well, Pa, Melvin up," Junie said with a sneer.

"No matter, Junie. We goin'. Get everythin' in de wagon," John said.

John then walked over to the men. "I gon' leave de fire going for ya. We be peaceable folk. But we not slaves. You can't take from us just 'cause ya say ya can. We thank ya kindly for de horses and de little bit of food and coins ya had. Dis c'here gun gon' sho' 'nuff come in handy, thou'. Now, I's gots two."

Melvin then looked shocked that John had a gun. "Yes, suh. I coulda shot ya. But I didn't. Tell de Lord, thank ya!"

Placing his hat on his head, John got up on the wagon seat with Sari and Junie. They could hear the yelling of one man and the muffled cries of the other as the wagon rolled away.

When they got to a better stretch of dirt trail, John put the reins down hard. He was wrapped head to toe, and the winter chill made Junie remark that he missed the warmth o' the smithy. John didn't stop except for the switching of the horses, leg stretches, and bathroom breaks until nightfall, and even Sari failed to voice one complaint on going such a distance in one day. Finally, when she got too tired, she asked Junie questions about what freedom would be like when they got to Colorado.

The trio had never dreamed before as a family. They had never dreamed before out loud, even to themselves. They wondered together what it would be like to be their own people. John cautioned them about the hard work ahead, but he shared he had saved some money, and they would buy a little place of their own.

"Papa, how you save so much coin?" Junie wanted to know because that was one part of their escape his father never shared. So Junie figured he'd find a job as a blacksmith when they got to their destination.

"I always had a little I made afta' every job outside de plantation. Massa . . . no. His name be Jacob. He send me out, and dey always want mo' when I get dere. I give half of de mo' to Jacob, and the other half I keep. Been saving since Sari girl get her womanly bits."

Sari's face went crimson red. "Papa!"

Junie looked at his papa, admiring him more than ever. "You'se a mighty good man, Papa. You was gon' run befo' the voice spoke?"

"Junie, I don' asked ya to call him what he is . . . angel. But I was gon' run or see if Donald would buy her for me or hav' her run. I couldn't let what happened to ya . . ." John's voice tapered off, and he did not complete his statement. He then started speaking again. "No, neva ya mind. Dat money gon' buy us our own place. Sari gon' find a good man to marry up wit' 'er. Junie, ya gon' make all types of coin for ya self. Life be open when ya be free."

Twenty-eight days later, the trio entered Colorado territory. It was not without additional challenges, however. But one thing the two thieving brothers had taught them was that together, they were formidable. Sari had not had one tantrum in the last three weeks. She had grown muscle, had a few callouses on her hands, and walked with a purposeful stride. Her long-legged gait was straight and true. To Junie's chagrin, she took to wearing pants as though it were natural.

Looking back, they had weathered the hard together. When they hit Missouri, they were once again in slave territory. However, they no longer felt like slaves. The timidity they had lived their lives with had begun to fall off with their successful defense of their own, and with each turn of the wagon's wheels and each mile they traveled, it grew. How do you stuff self-value back into a box too little to hold it? They had all grown.

And nearing St. Louis, they stayed on the outskirts of town but saw free people of color on the road. They had never seen free colored people out in the open like that, and soon, one older man pulled alongside them.

Slowing his mule instead of moving past as others had, the old man tipped his hat at Sari. "How do."

"How do, suh?"

"You folk travelin' far? You lookin' peaked. I'm freeman Willie Johnson. You welcome to follow me to my place. It's little, but it's warm, and I know my woman got something hot on the fire. Yaw's sho"nuff welcome."

Surprise written across John's face, he said, "Dats mighty nice of ya. I gon' kindly thank ya. De's children could use some heat."

Smiling brightly, Junie and Sari bounced with joy. Finally, they would see a free colored man's house!

Following behind, they entered a small patch of land with a small log home. It was a step above their cabin, and it looked snug and warm. Pulling around back, they unhitched the horses, and John commenced to rub them down. He then moved to water and feed them.

They saw Willie pumping water in a pail and motioning them to follow him while John continued his duties. Junie and Sari followed.

"Mamie!" Willie called out as they entered a small kitchen.

A large woman, taller and broader than Willie, bustled into the room, "Oh my, just like ya, man. Ya brang me company wit' no notice at t'all." She looked at Sari and rolled right over to her. "Poor thang. Ya look like dey don rode ya hard, chile. Come to Mamie, darlin'."

Sari was pulled into her warmth. "I's Sari, ma'am."

Mamie tilted Sari's chin up and said, "Yes, ya is." She then looked over to Junie and held her arms out. "And who dis strapping boy-man?"

Junie reluctantly went into her arms. Her warmth reminded him too much of Cinda and the gaping hole missing her had left in him. But Mr. Willie was so nice to invite them in, and it was so warm inside, he didn't want to disrespect anyone.

Reading his hesitancy and stepping back, Mamie kept her smile bright. "I 'spect a man-chile like ya might be too big for being coddled. But I bet some good food to ya ribs gon' brang a smile to ya face."

Junie smiled then, and when the door opened, and his father walked in, he brightened even more.

"Da more, da merrier! How do ya, suh? I'm Mamie," Mamie said as she went over to the cook fire in the hearth and put more logs on.

Taking his hat from his head, John bowed his head. "How do, ma'am. I thank ya and Mr. Willie fa' lettin' us be here fa' a short while."

Snorting, Willie said, "Y'all gon' stay the night. We gon' give ya a good hot meal, and ya can bed down in c'here. Ya ain't the first we helped along the way, and you won't be the last. One day, we hope it ain't gon' be necessuhry, but till den, we got ya."

Mamie stirred the pot on the stove top. "Willie, let Tillie know I could use a little of that pork I gave her last month back. We want them to have something to stick to their ribs."

Willie went back to the hook on the wall and put on his coat again. Then he wrapped his scarf around his neck and ventured back out the door.

"How can I help? I can chop wood fa' ya. Fetch mo' water?" John asked, not used to idleness.

Mamie placed her hands on her hips. "You can sat yaself down, Mr. John. How long it been since ya just sat a spell?"

"Neva, ma'am."

Junie rubbed his hands together because it smelled so delicious, and the household warmth felt so good. The hearth's warmth heated the entire tiny house. Looking around, he could see a parlor and another room on the other side that must be their bedroom. Mamie saw him looking around and flicked her hand for him to go explore.

When Junie walked into the front room, he saw a bedroom off; although not much, it was more than he saw any Black person have to themselves. They could sit here, or there, or over in the kitchen. They even had two windows.

Junie leaned back in the chair. He noted his father and Sari both relaxed and sitting in comfort. His father's hair was now speckled grey at the temples.

When did that happen?

Sometimes in the wagon at night, he heard his father get up and walk around, making sure that everything was all right. He rested little, and he had become haggard over the last weeks. They needed this rest.

Suddenly, the door burst open, and Mr. Willie walked in, almost prancing in his glee. "Mamie, get a skillet ready. Tillie gave us a nice fat chicken and the pork. Amos unloaded big freight on the docks yestidy, and they feelin' blessed to share."

Mamie began moving around the kitchen in rapid flair. A good chicken, greens, and ham was gon' be a mighty good meal. She placed cornmeal on the table. Working with Cinda in the kitchen so much, Junie knew the hot water cornbread would make the meal perfect.

Later, humming as he pinched his fingers from the corn bread to the greens, mouth greasy and stomach filled, Junie leaned back and burped loudly.

Mamie giggled. "Yes'm, now I *know* it's good."

John arched his eyebrow at Junie.

"'Cuse me, please," Junie said, talking through a Cheshire grin. Willie stretched and stood. "Outhouse out back, and if ya bring in more water, Mamie will heat it up so everyone can get at least a good bath 'fore you go to sleep. Bring ya bedrolls in. A rope runs from here to the outhouse if it's too dark to see, but there's a lantern right by the door."

"A bath—not a pot of heated water but a bath!" Sari hugged Mamie and danced around the room.

She helped Mamie hang the blanket in front of the large tub that John brought in, and Junie carried in their bedrolls.

As Sari bathed, Mamie called John and Junie to her. Her eyes peered intently at both, young and old. Then taking a deep breath, she grabbed their hands in hers. "Come brang me my Bible, Willie."

Junie gasped. "Ya got da Lord's word, Ms. Mamie? Ya can read?"

"I's read a little, but Wisdom, a free man hereby, is teachin' all of us. And I don' put in my heart da words I mean to live by."

Willie came and stood next to Mamie. She put both father and son's hands to rest on the Bible. She cocked her ear and noted that Sari was still happily bathing by her off-key singing and intermittent splashes of water. "Dis c'here a special boy, and you both on a special mission from God Himself. He spoke to me in my dreams last night, and that's why I axed ya to stay one mo' day. But I didn't and don't understand what I'm seeing. So, I'm just gon' tell ya, ya in God's hands, and He alone knows your future. So, be not afraid; your steps be ordered."

Junie thought of the crazy things he had seen earlier. "Ms. Mamie?"

"Yes, chile?"

Junie gulped, and then he leaned forward and whispered, "Did ya see peoples in boxes movin' around? And ... and long, smooth roads wit' different-shaped and colored boxes, people in dem? Scares me, Auntie."

Stepping back, Mamie placed her hand on her chest. "My God! You is so special, boy. In da days ahead, when ya not sho', lead anyhow. Listen and do. The Lord spoke to a child when man wouldn't listen. Ya got dat Jeremiah spirit on ya."

Puzzled, John asked, "Ya didn' hav' Sari put her hand on da Bible, Ms. Mamie. Why tell?"

"'Cause God didn't tell me to do it with her. Dats why." Mamie gave an audible breath in and out. "But fear not. Where ya go, she go. Ya lead. She now know to follow. Spirit showed me foolishness was her friend. She changin' now; be mo' different later. Somebody who loved her special turned her ear. She ain't as daft as she show, but she be foolish in dat she embraced low thinkin'. It got good to her. She got a role, but God say He gon' reveal it later."

John nodded his head. "I's 'ppreciate ya words. I gon' study on it."

Mamie put her hands on her wide hips. "Humph! Study or not, what's true is true. Now, I gon' check on ya girl-child. Some grown woman business is needed."

Stomping behind the curtain, Mamie looked at Sari slumped into the water, turning cold. Sari had a slight smile on her face. "Wake up dere, fast tail gal."

Sari jumped, bringing her rag to cover her womanly assets. "Oh, Auntie, ya plumb scared me."

"I scared ya? Or dat dere man in ya dream?"

Eyes wide as an owl's, Sari blinked, lost for words. "I . . . I . . ."

"I, ain't gon' help ya. Man in ya spirit. Be that way with some folk. Love tap dem on da shoulder, and when dey answer, dey forever stuck. Some time it be good love. Sometime if be bad, toothache-hurtin' bad. But man so tight in ya heart, you won't get dat bad tooth pulled."

"I . . . I . . ."

"Lord, chile. Spit it out or swallow it!"

Whispering, Sari murmured, "Neva met him, ma'am. Rides my dreams for a while now."

"He a haint?" Mamie said, shocked.

"No, no. Not a haint. Just in my dreams, not my life."

"Hmmmm. Dis be new. What be wrong wit' dis man?"

Blushing, Sari reached out for the towel. Mamie reached it first, and hung in it front of her so she could climb out of the rub. Her head down, Sari whimpered, "He be white."

Breathing in and out, Mamie stumbled and sat. "It ain't new. But it ain't neva been pretty. I gon' pray God has a ram in da bush fa ya. Some thangs ya can only pray 'bout."

Sari slipped into her clothing. "Pray hard, Auntie. 'Cause I don' tried, but the dreams keep coming."

"I's on one accord wit' ya. And listen, ya stop playin' wit' folk. Whateva ya did before to make it? Loose dat thang now. Be the real ya. Anythang else kin to witchcraft. What somebody meant for ya good, devil don' made it for his good."

Startled, Sari looked up for a long time. She then exhaled, nodded her head, and left from behind the curtain. On the other side of the quilt, those in the room could hear Mamie break out in a spiritual that stilled them all in reverence. The spirit was moving.

After all their baths and a good night's sleep, morning came. They left with their bellies full of food and encouraged that God was their conductor, whatever came.

Willie and Mamie showed them what freedom looked like up front, and, in turn, they promised to be of help to others whenever they could. Their two-day stay was the boon they needed to finish their race. They were blessed with replenished supplies from the free Black community in this small corner of St. Louis, Missouri. The residents had learned to survive together.

Back on the road, the trials continued, but they remained courageous. They encountered more thieves, but the brothers proved the worst. John had to shoot his gun but failed to hit anything. It did send a message, though, that they would not be easy prey, and those looking for easy moved on. There were days when the cold and snow slowed them down to a crawl, and they thought they would never get there. They huddled at night for warmth, and their campfire stayed stoked nightly. Heated bricks were inserted in clothing, and John showed truth as real strength as he spoke words of love and encouragement, not anger or defeat, to get them through each day.

Junie knew God worked in mysterious ways, the way He sent those thieves after them, but instead, they got two more horses and a gun. When they hit the snow, they used all six animals to get them through. And they kept going—nothing else to do.

Junie looked down at his piece of wood, twenty-nine notches. A month and they were entering Colorado Springs. Only the almighty God could have brought them so far.

John slowed the horses and looked up at the mountains. "It's beautiful."

Sari and Junie shared a smile as they sniffed the clear, fresh air.

John stopped the wagon, and Junie got out and cupped his hands around his mouth, and yelled, "Hello . . ."

"Hello, hello," echoed all around him.

John clapped his hands in jubilation with his children. Then he stopped and looked up. "Get in de wagon! Hurry, hurry," he yelled frantically.

Junie and Sari both jumped in, and John slapped those reins harder than he ever had. The horses, already skittish, took off. Faster and faster they went as they all saw the snow roaring toward them from their right side. Sweat popped off their foreheads, hands clenched, and the muscles in John's arms bulged.

"Hee-yah, hee-yah!" John screamed as they tumbled up the road.

But the snow was faster, harsher, determined, and all that white was headed for them!

"Papa!" Sari yelled as the snow met her and cut off her breath.

Junie's last thought as he closed his eyes was, *Keep us, God.*

Looking from a panoramic view, you could see the horses disappear; then John, Sari, and Junie. Then the wagon. Nothing but white . . . all gone.

Avalanche.

Chapter Nine

Present

Zachary tread up the hallway in the executive suites of Burstein Labs. His forehead protruded as its veins pulsed with anger. If his mother hadn't drummed into him that cursing was a lazy man's vocabulary, he would be spewing the foulest language he could think of, learned from the hardest, meanest men in the United States Army. He wanted—no, he needed—some answers. He was nobody's puppet dancing to an invisible hand they had stuck up his butt!

He was told to have his best men waiting, and then they had the unmitigated gall to come back incognito and failed to contact him. So he was in the dark. How could he secure what he didn't even know existed?

How 'bout I kick this job or your butt—or both?

As he approached the CEO's office door, it swung open. Dressed impeccably, Edgar Burstein glided past Zachary as though he had ordered him there instead of him showing up unexpectedly for some answers. It was typical. He was as arrogant as always.

"Good, good, glad you're here. Follow me and have your best men meet me in the basement labs. This is so exciting."

Zachary touched the device in his ear and advised his men to meet him in the basement. "You don't usually do any business on this floor, sir. Can I ask why now?" he said in a terse voice, his eye now twitching in an effort to keep his mouth from signing a check he wasn't ready to cash.

Moving swiftly through the halls, Edgar said, "The basement is not just a research lab. It is also a medical clinic. It is as large as the entire building. We will need every inch of space to do what we have determined is necessary."

Zachary made long strides keeping up and then asked, "And what would that be, sir?"

Edgar hesitated, then nodded as if making a spur-of-the-moment decision to let Zachary in finally. "Save their lives."

Arriving at the elevator, Zachary pushed the button, then stood back as it opened. He placed his arm over the door's closing mechanism and went in after his boss. Touching the basement button, Edgar reached across him and hit the red star button *below* the basement button.

Breathing out heavy, Zachary squared his shoulders. Looking into the gleaming steel of the panel, he could see his reflection. He knew he looked like he felt . . . pissed off. There was another level to this building that he had no clue about? The basement wasn't *really* the basement? He looked ahead when the executive elevator opened first on the basement level he pushed.

There stood his men assembled in the lobby in front of the labs. "Get on, men," he barked.

The men climbed on as Bebop stood next to him, nudging his shoulder, letting him know he understood something was up.

The elevator descended instead of moving up, and Zachary's trained men stiffened but wisely did not open their mouths. When the doors slid open, Bebop jumped out, moved to the side, and held his arm in front of the sliding door. Zachary's men moved in military precision as they filed out, Zachary being the last before Edgar to exit the elevator. As Edgar came out, he moved with arrogance between the men who had formed a protective row on either side of him.

Getting to the front of the line, Edgar swept his arm toward a door. "After you, gentlemen."

The men silently filed into a plush conference room. An older blond woman walked around the table. There were six folders placed one before each chair circling the table.

Zachary nodded for his men to sit before each offering.

Edgar stood at the head of the table and looked at each security officer. "These are your best?" he asked as he unbuttoned his custom suit and paced at the head of the table. Then, not waiting for Zachary to answer, he said, "I notice my cousin, Tom, is not among them. Good choice. He's an idiot but family."

Zachary stayed quiet. What could he say? Maybe Edgar was able to offer truth after all.

Edgar gave a slight nod to the woman standing next to him. "This is my most able executive assistant, Marilyn. She has placed some very important documents in front of each of you to sign."

Stoic, Zachary thought, *Now, where did she come from?*

Marilyn leaned forward. "If you open your folders, the first form is a new updated nondisclosure agreement. This NDA is not a standard agreement. To sign this is to state that you will not only be held legally liable but financially as well. In other words, gentlemen, you may not share any information with your wives, mothers, cousins, or boo thang. You may not even share your assignments with each other. Do we all understand?"

Bebop stood at attention. "Ma'am, may I speak frankly?"

"Yes, of course."

"Are you saying we cannot share this information with even our top command, Security Chief Trumbull?"

Zachary was ready to hear the answer to that himself. He could not believe that they were going this far. They had already signed an NDA at hire. What was so top secret that they were being made to sign a new, more stringent document?

And boo thang. Really?

Edgar held up his hand for Marilyn to let him handle the answer. "Officer," then he read Bebop's name badge and completed his address, "William, for this special assignment and in all things Burstein Labs, *I* am your top command. Have I made myself clear?"

"Roger that," Bebop said and took his seat.

"The second sheet is a conflict of interest form. If you are part of any group, have strong political affiliations or worldviews that would make you hesitant to follow orders, please do not sign this form. You are instead excused from this group, although you will be allowed to maintain your employment."

Bebop again stood. Looking around, he shrugged his shoulders. "Sorry to seem like I have so many questions, but what do you mean by special group affiliations or worldviews? Make it plain, please, sir."

Again, Edgar intercepted Marilyn's answer. "I like your spunk. You're not afraid to ask questions, even if they may make you appear to be a very stupid man. So, I'll answer for you. Groups like *Black Lives Matter, the NAACP, and UNCF*. Is that plain enough for you?"

Zachary wanted to know why these particular examples were used. After all, what did the United Negro College Fund have to do with Burstein Labs? And was he insulting Black folk or just Bebop?

Bebop, ever cool, sat back down. "Thank you, sir; no problem." He then promptly signed both papers.

Marilyn then went around the room and took each folder from the officers. "Thank you, gentlemen. Mr. Edgar Burstein, your CEO, will conduct the rest of this meeting."

Okay, that's overstating, Zachary thought.

"Zachary, I need your two most reliable men assigned inside the medical clinic, then the labs. They will work twelve-hour shifts and cover our esteemed guests to ensure they can recover with no outside interference."

"Yes, sir. That will be Officers William Thornton and Nelson Sloan. They will get the job done, sir."

Edgar stared at Bebop, hesitated, then replied, "All right, Zachary. I'm trusting you to know what you're doing. If they fail, you've failed."

"Of course," Zachary said. "I wouldn't have it any other way."

Edgar opened his mouth but then shrugged as he rebuttoned his suit coat. "Gentlemen, the other three of you, including your esteemed chief, Zachary, will secure the outer hallways and living quarters for staff. Those of you on hallway duty are free to go home daily. Those assigned inside the clinic and labs will remain here until further notice."

Bebop rolled his eyes at Zachary at this unexpected news. "Request to call home, sir."

Exasperated, Edgar scoffed. "Your cell phones will not work on this level of the building. You may only use the phone in this room, which is monitored at all times. Remember the NDAs you signed just twenty minutes ago. And if that doesn't help you, know that I *will* send you to hell on fire if you fail this mission."

Eyebrows arched, Zachary nodded to Bebop and Officer Sloan. "Make your calls and then go to your assignments. I'll check in with you every change of shift by this phone."

He then nodded to Bebop, blinking several times.

Zachary and his other three men moved into the hallway, with Edgar following.

As the men moved into position, Edgar walked Zachary to the elevator. "Sir, I am still unaware of just what we are guarding. I can be more of an asset if I am just made aware of what is really going on."

Edgar patted Zachary on the back. "That's the beauty of this whole plan, Zachary. The right hand doesn't need to know what the left hand is doing. But I am the brain that controls both hands. It works. Just do your job."

The elevator opened, and Zachary slid in. When he turned around to hit the up button, Edgar smiled. "And please tell that beautiful wife of yours I said hello."

Stupefied, Zachary looked into the condescending sneer of the biggest jerk he had ever had the misfortune of encountering as the doors slid closed. Always in control, Zachary kept his body fluid and his movements natural. He then looked down and screamed one word, efficiently breaking his mother's rule and projecting a *very* lazy vocabulary.

Chapter Ten

Present

Monitors flashed and beeped as white-coated personnel ran to and fro, mumbling about the miracle they witnessed as they adjusted knobs and fluid levels. Three people, large, slender, and small, with numerous tubes flowing from several areas of their bodies, were laid out in separate cylinder glass cubicles.

Zachary watched from the tiny eagle pin in Bebop's tie that was not only a high-tech camera but also a wireless video. Zachary was grateful for his boys in Special Ops. Unfortunately, what he couldn't get at such short notice was video sound. So he watched the silent picture and worked his mind overtime to figure out what he was watching.

What's so special about these people, he wondered, *and where did they come from?*

Bebop inched forward, puffing out his chest so that Zachary could see as much as his range would allow. Zachary was stumped. But he taped everything to review later at home in his garage, away from Sylvia's prying eyes. One thing he never had to worry about was her caring what he did at home.

Slamming the door, Zachary called out, "Sylvia, I'm home! Sylvia . . ."

She didn't answer, and when Zachary entered his bedroom, he found her discarded outfits haphazardly strewn over the door, a chair, and the bed. She had obviously dressed to impress and gone out.

Good. Gives me time to grab something to eat and then go out to the garage and try to figure this out.

Zachary fixed a sandwich piled high with turkey, pickles, tomatoes, and lettuce, then placed a handful of baked chips on the side of a flimsy paper plate. Then grabbing his unsweetened iced tea and striding to the attached garage, he laid down his burdens, took a jump drive out of his pocket, and slid it into his laptop's port. As it powered up, he took a large bite out of his sandwich.

Come on, baby; help daddy with the answers daddy needs.

Zachary zoomed the screen close on each body.

Well, I'll be. They're all Black. What is Burstein Labs doing with what looks like a family of Black people?

Zachary then went to his search engine and began to search the last year for any missing family of Black people.

Nothing, or maybe he should say too many. Most were children, women, and men, but none related. *Is anybody looking for all these people?*

He clicked a few more buttons and went back two more years.

Still nothing, but more of the same. I don't remember seeing any of these people on the news.

Zachary chewed on his lower lip, a habit from childhood when he was thinking hard. He then Googled recent news.

Nope, just more blame and pointing fingers.

Finishing his makeshift meal, he clomped into the house and threw himself on the couch. Then picking up the remote, he turned on the television for white noise.

A young reporter looking straight out of media school with a Colgate-white smile chirped, *"In today's news, the climate group, A Better Tomorrow, continues to protest the fracking here in the Colorado mountains. One of their spokesmen, Gretchen Gaines, is here to express her concerns."*

Glancing up, Zachary saw the reporter thrust the microphone under Gretchen's nose. The young woman gently brought the mic down to mouth level and spoke. *"I'm here on behalf of every person on this planet who believes their children's children should be able to breathe clean air, drink clean water, and live in a land not ravaged by earthquakes, landslides, forest fires, and hurricanes. Fracking is wrong!"*

Nodding and thrusting the microphone even harder into her personal space, the female reporter asked, *"But what was the breaking news you saw? Give us the secret Benson Industries is hiding!"*

Gulping, Gretchen looked startled at the ferocity of her questioning. *"It's . . . it's . . . bla—sssssh."*

Zachary clicked the remote to clear the white snow that had suddenly filled the screen. He clicked forward and saw the next channel was clear, the sound was crisp. He clicked back, and the white snow persisted on channel eight. "Strange."

Zachary clicked the channel back and forth again. A different newscaster suddenly appeared on the channel.

"We are back," he said, holding his earpiece, his voice chirpy. *"Thank you for your patience. Unfortunately, here in the mountains, our broadcasts can receive interference. Now, back to our news story."*

Leaning forward, Zachary was interested in what the reporter was going to say when a different female reporter sat at her desk and smiled brightly into the camera. *"Channel Eight's policy is always to bring you the truth when you need it and where you want it. In keeping with this policy, we are sorry to advise that our last interviewee has proven inaccurate, based on comments from a false witness. Her statement has unsubstantiated conspiracy theory stamped all over it. We hope to bring you more 'real' news live at our seven a.m. newscast. Our broadcast from the Benson Industries site will now continue with Chuck Winston, our star reporter arriving on the scene. Chuck, we're now to you."*

Chuck, looking unprepared and startled as the camera swung to him, stammered over his words as he fiddled with his hood and exclaimed, *"The weather here is very cold, folks. So, as you can see, this is the perfect place for your kids to have a snowball fight . . ."*

Did this yahoo just tell parents to have their kids have a snowball fight in the middle of the night?

Flipping the channel away from the weirdest news show he had seen in a while, Zachary settled in, and the television was soon watching him instead of him watching it. His napping was interrupted by the sound of a key in the front door lock. Knowing that Sylvia was the only person who would be coming in, he sat up and took a deep breath.

Eeny meeny miny moe, which Sylvia today is gonna show?

"Did I ever care? Why are you laid up on my good couch? With your shoes on?" Sylvia blasted as she placed her keys in the bowl in the foyer. "You have a television in the garage, and there's the guest room if you want to lounge around. We will never have anything if you continue to treat good things as worthless."

Zachary had stopped listening as soon as he heard the use and tone of his name on her lips. His question had been answered. *And the winner for two hundred is . . . Witch!*

Zachary looked at his phone. It was way past midnight. "It's after 2:00 a.m., Sylvia. Where've you been?"

"Minding my own business."

Zachary mused with a drawl. "My mama taught me an important reality long ago: the only thing open after two in the morning is legs or hotels." He slowly let his eyes drift from her tousled hair to the stilettos in her hands. "Ding, ding, ding, the prize for a bull's eye goes to the woman who has her own house, so it must have been door number two; Her legs were—"

Loud hand claps crescendoed over Zachary's accusations. "Thanks for a great performance made by a husband who gives a crap. But, honey, if you cared, I might try to hear you, but we both know you stopped caring about my whereabouts long ago."

Sylvia calmly placed her shoes neatly by the door and sauntered the rest of the way toward their room. Zachary stood and cut her off from strolling down the arched hallway.

Clasping her upper arm, he asked, "And you, Sylvia? When did *you* stop caring?"

Snatching her arm from his grasp, Sylvia looked deep into Zachary's steeled glare. "Wrong question, Soldier Boy."

Zachary looked at her, puzzled. Then, shrugging, he said, "Okay, I'll bite. What's the *correct* question?"

Jeering, Sylvia moved farther down the hall. Looking back over her shoulder, she quipped, "Did I *ever* care, Zachary?"

Stepping through the doorway, she quietly closed the door, and he heard the faint sound of the bedroom door locking. That soft click resounded through his integrity, ricocheted off his loyalty, and landed in his resolve. In his heart, his marriage that had been on a ventilator—had just lost any signs of life.

He wondered which one would be brave enough to pull the plug and give the time of death.

Chapter Eleven

Zachary twirled his pen between his fingers as he sat at his desk, staring into space. He had such a vivid dream about the green-eyed girl last night that he tossed and turned into dawn. He did notice one thing, though. In the past, the dreams always seemed like she was far away, more like at the end of a tunnel. But in this dream, she was close up, but all around her was dark, except for her green eyes and the sheen of desperation in them. The dreams were back and in cinematic color. He didn't know how he ever thought Sylvia could have been the woman in them. Yes, she had green eyes ... enhanced by vivid green contacts, but the glow of intelligence and an inner burning fire had always been missing. He had mistaken cunning for intelligence, desperation for adoration. He wouldn't be fooled again. And until he buried the corpse of his marriage, he was beholden to stay a man of honor, even if eyes of jade followed him through his dreams.

Shaking himself conscious, he picked up the ringing phone. "Burstein Labs, Chief of Security, Zachary Trumbull speaking." Zachary listened, then stood while holding the phone. "Yes, I can be there right away. Roger that, sir."

Zachary immediately left his office and bumped into Bebop, who was leaning on the wall in an alcove right before the elevator. Bebop pointed up to the camera, right over his head. Zachary approached as though hitting the elevator button but instead slid next to Bebop, where they were side by side, under the camera.

Bebop whispered, "It took me this long to figure a way to get up here without all the new cameras catching me."

Zachary nodded, but before they started the much-needed conversation, he checked up and down the hall. Eight days had passed, four since he had spoken to Bebop or received any transmissions.

"I been more than worried, bro," Zachary murmured. "Speed dial it to me."

Bebop quickly reported that the family had been moved to a newly constructed, much-larger lab. He continued to be the guard, but there were some kinds of buffers inside of it that made it impossible to send any feed to Zachary. He had not been allowed to leave during the transfer or even contact his family. HR got in touch with his wife, Belinda. He was advised that he would need to stay in the dorm for the next few months, and communication with anyone outside of the lab was forbidden. He would be paid triple his salary. They were talking about instituting a family day, where guards' families could come up to visit, but that had not been confirmed.

"None of this was run by me. Man, I'm sorry," Zachary bemoaned after hearing how far Edgar had gone in his directives to keep things quiet.

Bebop's eyes narrowed. "You're sorry? Man, I might already be on my way to divorce court and not know it. How much you bet that Big Brother will monitor any visits? I did *not* sign up for this mess!"

Zachary winced at the fervor coming at him from his friend, along with some spittle he was trying to duck. "I hear you, man. But at this point, things are so out of bounds that I'm not sure if you or your family would be safe if you left."

"Dude, I will *kill* some folk up in here over mine," Bebop sputtered.

Zachary nodded. "And I'd help. But look, I was on my way to Edgar's office. So let me get going, and then I will find a way to talk to you again today."

This is such bull! Why leave me out?

Leaving the elevator and knocking on Edgar Burstein's office door that had been temporarily moved to this floor, Zachary heard the command to enter.

Standing erect in front of Edgar's desk, Zachary almost saluted; instead, he cleared his throat and said, "Yes, sir. How may I be of service?"

"I have just learned that one of your top picks has fallen and broken his leg. I will need a new guard assigned to take his place. Please see to it posthaste. Make sure it is someone discrete. They will also be made to wear a particular uniform of our choosing, none of which this person may be at liberty to share with anyone. Including you. Do I make myself clear?"

"Yes, sir. I will get on that right away. Where will you have them report, sir?"

"Have them relieve the current man on duty at the changing of shifts. He will meet my assistant, Marilyn, the woman you guys met at the beginning of this project. She will meet him at the elevator furthest down the hall and take him to his checkpoint."

"The freight elevator, sir?"

"Yes. That will be all," Edgar stated as he resumed reading a large leather-bound book, turning the pages deliberately with his finger running down each page.

Zachary tried to read upside down to see what held Edgar's interest, but he was never good at it. All he could make out were the words "HeLa" and "cells." Frustrated, he inched closer when Edgar looked up from his deliberations.

Pulling off his glasses, he glared at Zachary with pure annoyance. "Is there a problem?"

Rolling his eyes in frustration, he said, "No, no problem."

"Then I suggest you do the difficult task of putting one foot in front of the other and completing the order you were called here to do."

Zachary paused, then, in military formation, stepped forward. "Sir, if I may say so, it would be much easier for me to take command of my team, which will allow you to do the heavy lifting you need to do to secure the success of this project."

Folding and unfolding his glasses, Edgar gave a long sigh. "Things were going so well. Then like the scarecrow in *The Wiz*, you decided that you had a brain. Hear me when I say *I* can do your job and twenty others in this company without breaking a sweat. You would do well to competently fulfill what I have asked you to do and look to taking care of your own life and home." Placing his glasses back on his Roman nose, Edgar leaned down and continued reading. Without looking up again, he shooed Zachary out of his office. "Good day. Close the door on your way out."

He had been dismissed . . . turned out like a schoolboy who was asking to go out during recess.

Zachary briskly walked up the hall. *Does he not understand that I know twenty ways to kill a man?* Zachary thought about telling him to take the job and shove it. *Doggone it, a man who is on the verge of divorce can't afford to be broke, and I got Bebop into this . . .* Zachary's inner tirade skidded to a stop. *On the other hand, what I don't have, the court can't take, and Bebop is getting paid triple what he was making.*

After taking the elevator up to his office, he called his assistant, Tom. "Morning. I'm making some changes to today's schedule. As you probably already know, we've got a broken leg issue, so we'll need another guard to replace him posthaste. Either McConnell or Murphy will do."

The phone was silent while Zachary waited for affirmation from Tom on the changes.

Then with a reticent tone, Tom said, "I know I make mistakes. But you can trust me, Chief. I'm hashtag Team Zachary."

Pulling the phone receiver away from his face, Zachary frowned. "Hashtag Team Zachary?"

"Just because the kids don't act like they know the parents are fighting doesn't mean the kids don't know. It's the talk of the building. My butthole of a cousin doesn't trust you to lead whatever top-secret operation we're now in the middle of—"

"—You are very close to insubordination, Tom. The rumors are just that, and let's get this straight. I'm *not* your daddy."

"Yes, sir! I understand, sir."

Zachary hung up the phone. *Why do I know that fool was saluting the phone?*

Bill, better known to those who served with him as Bebop, sat forward in the chair in the dorm room, his hands in steeple mode.

"I'm not sure what's going on. They were in those cylinder thingamajigs for about four days. Then they did the transfer to the larger lab. This lab is like some kind of spaceship-type getup . . . all kinda wires and tubing coming out of everywhere, feeding them all kinds of solutions, and then monitoring them on several large beeping machines." Bebop rubbed his hands over his face. "Get this, I tried transmitting to you, and some kind of red light went off in the corner, but I saw it, right? Man, I had to hurry to the bathroom and flush the transmitter down the toilet. When I came back, Edgar was there asking all of us to empty our pockets, and the Marilyn lady wands us!"

"Dang it," Zachary swore.

"Nah, man. Dang it don't get it. When Marilyn wands me, I see the piece under her blazer. Marilyn is more than just his executive assistant. The gun made me note how she stood and the steel in her grip when she turned me around while checking me. And if you look closely, she's not that old. It's the makeup and hairstyle. I'm telling you, nothing about this feels right."

Zachary held out his hand and ticked off his fingers. "Three Black people, a man, a younger woman, and a boy, that much we know. All being given top-notch attention with the highest secrecy. And they are spending a lot of money on equipment and medical personnel. So whatever this is, it ain't kosher."

"Yeah, like fish, it stinks after two days."

Zachary grinned. "Kinda like this dorm room."

"You *don't* want to know some of these dudes' habits—straight-up nasty. I miss my family. We need to get to the bottom of this because I miss my wife's bottom. Day-old shoe funk is *not* my idea of a great sleeping environment."

"I'm doing what I can. In the meantime, we'll keep meeting here. I'm surprised they haven't placed cameras in here."

"Oh, they did. Tom helped me out with that one. He changes the picture every couple of hours," Bebop said, laughing.

"Man, no way. My bumbling assistant?"

"Yeah. He approached me about being hashtag Team Zachary. Apparently, his cousin-in-law had bullied him since he came into the family when Tom entered his teens. He's hated him ever since. It runs deep, man. I think he only took this job to get him somehow."

Zachary rubbed his chin, and his eyes gleamed. "We can use that."

Bebop clasped his hands together and rubbed them. "The enemy of my enemy and all that jazz?"

"Yeah, man. And although we can't use Morse code here, since we aren't the only ex-military, we can make up our own codes and signals in case we need to communicate a dire warning."

Bebop gave Zachary a fist dap. "Yes, sir, let's get that popping. And let's find out what kind of mess the mighty Edgar is pulling on these poor folk." Bebop then rubbed his stomach. "Yeah, and then let me get home to my family. I don't know about you, but I don't fly well when I don't get some loving. Brother kinda hungry."

"Yeah, well, try starving!" Zachary said, knowing neither was talking about food.

Bebop grimaced. "You had enough yet?"

"Humph, I just said I'm *starving*." Zachary stood to leave.

"What that young rapper, J Cole say, 'Cold World, No Blanket?'"

Zachary leaned toward his friend and punched him in the shoulder. "You so wrong for that. Right, but so wrong."

Rubbing the now-sore spot, Bebop almost pleaded, "Then when all this is over, make it happen, man. It's beyond time to shake loose from that bondage. You not even a religious man to stay in a marriage because you believe it's the right thing to do. It's either madness or cowardness. And I never saw you as a coward." Bebop used air quotes when he spoke the word "coward."

Zachary shuddered. "I always tell you that integrity does not always line up with religion. Some of the worst acts of violence in history have been condoned by the church. So I'll pass, thank you. And I got your coward right here." Zachary grabbed himself intimately.

"Nah, man, keep them moves for your bedroom." Bebop sighed, then reasoned, "Church folk don't mean saved folk. You should know that by now. How many churches did me and Belinda have to leave before we found one that preached the unadulterated word of God?"

"I hate to interrupt your station identification for your push to have me accept salvation, but I need to go, and I need to think."

"Yeah, you running on empty to grab your crotch and then punch me. You need a Calgon bath or a hug. And I got neither. I'll get with you on prime time," Bebop said while pointing his finger for Zachary to leave the room. "I'ma need prayer after talking to you."

While you at it, hit up your Lord for a little divine intervention.

Chapter Twelve

Zachary Googled the words "HeLa cells" and keyed as fast as his fingers would go as his mind raced. He couldn't believe the number of references that exploded on his laptop. He had never heard any of this, and here were pages and pages popping up about an African American woman named Henrietta Lacks.

They're fighting to teach Critical Race Theory in the schools, and important basic history we're not learning because of the melanin in somebody's complexion? This is straight-up bull. The woman literally was responsible for saving millions of lives.

From what he was reading, she had cancer, and her cancerous cells were sent from John Hopkins Hospital for scientific research in 1951. Later, tragically she herself died from the disease.

Wow, she was only thirty-one.

Unknown to her, and it appeared in a routine process, her cells were sent for research. When the lab discovered her cells were not dying like the rest of the cancerous cells they received but actually were multiplying, they were floored. The facts were that the cells were immortal, and they used them for the basis of what we now know as modern medicine. Her HeLa cells were used to create treatments for cancer, immunology, and infectious diseases. More recently, they had even been used for the basis of COVID-19 vaccines.

Zachary rubbed his eyes in frustration. *So why is Edgar studying HeLa cells?*

Ears always tuned, he heard a car pull up outside the garage door. He knew the car door opened because he could hear the Country and Western song pouring from it before the music stopped and a door slammed shut. The clicking of heels left no doubt who had arrived.

Moaning, he closed his laptop and locked it inside his old metal desk. He then went into the house, halting his entrance at the door. There, in front of him, was a pathetic spectacle. Perched on the arm of the chair, wobbling as though she were on the cusp of pitching face forward, was his most beloved wife. Sylvia's hair was wrecked in a punk-spiked look that he was convinced she had not left the house with, and her eyes were red-rimmed. She looked as though she had fought with the Tasmanian devil and, as a result, lost her soul.

Did demons have a soul? Unfortunately, it was too late for examinations best done *before* you tied the knot. His only recourse was to reroute this marriage's suicide mission.

Sylvia slid onto the couch, her legs splayed wide open. She arched her brows and puckered her lips as though she looked enticing. Regrettably, her attempt was disrupted by her loud belch that filled the entryway with noxious fumes and the dribble escaping from the corner of her filler-injected blubbery lips.

Stopping directly in front of her, Zachary didn't even try to remove the disgust from his tone. "Woman, you drinking this early in the evening?"

Sliding further down to the floor, she burped, then giggled. "I'm not sure why you are even bothering to talk to me, Zachary. You're immune to my charm," she slurred.

Ignoring her statement, he lamented, "You're drunk, and you'll be sick in the morning."

"How 'bout, I'm sick of you now. Leave me alone, why don't you?" she whined as she stumbled up from the floor and propped herself against the wall.

Zachary strode over, intending to help, but when he looked down at her as she fought to stay upright, he stopped short of touching her. This close, he could smell an overpowering man's cologne. It was familiar, but he couldn't place why or where. Finally, plain tired, he deadpanned, "I want to leave you alone. I want to leave you—*period.*"

Placing her hands in mock prayer, she giggled. "Oh, goody. The Boy Scout finally makes a man move. Just remember, we never signed a prenup. And I won't go away with nothing. Mommy will need to be paid," Sylvia gayly explained. She then giggled again, singing an old rhythm and blues song over and over as she shook her narrow hips from side to side. "*It's cheaper to keep her.*"

"Sleep it off, Sylvia, and try to hit the toilet bowl in the morning. I'm not cleaning up after you again," Zachary growled as he marched down the hallway away from her juvenile antics, headed to the guest bedroom.

"*You* sleep it off," she yelled after him. Then Zachary heard a bang, a crash, and her subsequent yell of pain as he slowly grinned but refused to look back.

Zachary scowled, throwing what felt like a million pillows from the guest room's bed onto the leather recliner.

Why do women have all these pillows no one is allowed to lie on? To frustrate men, that's why.

Carefully rolling over on his back on the full-size bed, feet hanging over, he was mentally piecing things together from all he learned in his earlier research on Henrietta Lacks. None of the scenarios he came up with looked good for anyone involved. What he read on how the HeLa cells—named after its predecessor—came to be was such an invasion of a person's individual rights that he was appalled. Opening his phone, he Googled more.

Zachary couldn't understand how they got away with doing what they did to her. So he kept reading and finally read something called the Common Rule, meaning the medical profession had a right to do what they did. They had a right to take your cells; they had a right to not tell you about it. And they had a right to profit off of it. So, where was the right of the person who came to them with complete belief in them upholding their Hippocratic Oath that "thy will do no harm"?

Sounds like they were the only ones no harm came to.

Zachary wished he could thank Henrietta Lacks for all she had done in medical breakthroughs for everyone when she herself died of cancer. As he continued to read, he found some changes had been made in 2018 that revised the Common Rule, much too late and too little for the Lacks family.

And now, there were three bodies at Burstein Labs, three Black bodies. And whatever was being done to them, it was being done in secret. All his life, his parents had told him people were people, but he saw it time and time again that some people didn't matter to the world, in general. He had fought for his country, fought because he hated injustice anywhere. He wished he had his brother in arms, Legend, with him. He was always their strategist. He laid out the plan, and he made sure it was executed. But Legend had gone to the dark side . . . left the military to become a mercenary. Big money called to him stronger than big patriotism.

Zachary understood he couldn't solve this alone. He had to take a chance if he was going to find out what was happening to those people. He had to trust more than just Bebop. Resigned, he looked up a number in his contacts and tapped on it.

"Hello?"

"Tom, Zachary Trumbull here. I got your message from Bill. Are you positive you're willing to get involved in something that could get us all killed if the stakes are as high as I think they are?" he said, sitting at the end of the bed.

"I meant what I said. I'm hashtag Team Zachary. And—"

"—Come on, dude! Quit with the hashtag. It's just Security Chief Zachary Trumbull. Pick any of those titles or names and use them."

"Right. Got it. My assignment, sir?" Tom shouted.

Zachary groaned. "Inside voice, *pleasssse*. Can you get into Edgar's office to get any information you can find on something called HeLa cells? It was in a big leather-bound book he was reading. Might even be more files on it."

"Writing it down. How do you spell that?"

"Don't write it down. Remember it. Can you get it done?" Zachary questioned.

"I'll do you one better. I'll look in his home office tomorrow morning. My cousin will let me look. She's a sweetheart. She's always been good to me. She made that dictator hire me to keep the peace in the family. She knows he's had many affairs but can't get anything on him. Either the private detectives don't call back, or they just quit. But she's not willing to leave him after sixteen years of marriage without compensation for her pain and suffering, but because of her prenuptial agreement, she'll only get paid if she has had children or proof of infidelity. Since he made sure that no children would come in their second year of marriage with a vasectomy, she's left proving he's a cheater. The guy's a true slickster."

"Sorry for your cousin's predicament, but I'm concerned that lives are at stake. I just don't know for sure why."

Tom cleared his throat and spoke in a low, concise manner. "I can't say that if my cousin finally decides to leave Edgar, her life won't be in danger. I need to find something on him to keep her safe. You can count on me."

"All right then. No discussing any of this in the hallowed halls of work. We talk only on our personal cell phones. Be mindful of Marilyn. She's *not* who you think she is. *Never* drop your guard."

A dry chuckle came through the phone. "I'm pretty sure that at one point, Marilyn *was* the other woman, but she got replaced, that much I know. The fact that he didn't replace her in her position when their affair was over was more telling than anything. My cousin figured she had a skill beyond a regular assistant, one not easily duplicated. It's a shame they were so careful we could never get anything on them. She's one cool customer. A little old for my taste, though."

Zachary debated whether to tell Tom his suspicions concerning Marilyn . . . *screw it*. "Listen, like I said, she's not who she appears. She's around thirty to maybe thirty-five. Her makeup is obviously a cover not to draw attention to how attractive she really is and what her real position is working for Edgar. She was strapped, man, and it wasn't a cutesy piece. She also walks on the balls of her feet and moves with fluid precision. She's been trained in hand-to-hand."

"What the—?" Tom yelled.

"Duuude, stop with the yelling. What are you, a member of the yodeling commission? They heard you in the next county. Chill with the volume. I told you this information so you could realize that *nothing* is what it seems. Step light, and watch your back. It's me, you, and William. Trust no one else, not even your cousin."

Giving a loud "Roger that!" Tom crowed, "I got—" He hesitated, lowering his voice. "Oh, sorry about that. You and Bebop can rest assured, I got this."

Zachary closed his eyes and rolled his neck from side to side. "Right. Hit me up if you find anything—anything! You got it?"

"Yeah, man, on it."

"Oh, and lose the Bebop reference. He can be William until he lets you call him Bill. You may never get to Bebop. Later." Zachary hung up and flopped back on the bed.

Is any of this my business? What's pulling me in so hard to solve this? I'm paid to do nothing, literally. Zachary inched back, working on getting his entire body on the bed. He reached into the nightstand for a pad and paper.

Yeah, but Edgar thinks I'm a sucker, and I do hate getting played.

Pulling up HeLa cells on the web again, he settled in to try to figure out just how much he didn't know. He'd ponder an answer until he slept, and then he'd surrender his conscious to a love so pure that just touching her in his dreams was enough.

At least, for now . . .

Chapter Thirteen

Five Months Later

It was midnight ink without shadows, black with no relief . . . deep bleak gloom.

"Please please please."

Edges of memory tiptoed close to his consciousness. He pursued the awareness, remembrance close but never secure in his hands, the past fleeting through his fingers. He grappled, straining to pin down his life, to know the whys of his existence. Finally, he lay exhausted as he wrestled with an unknown foe imprisoned in his consciousness.

"Please, please."

The struggle was endless, with no clocks measuring time or a stopwatch to call the ordeal done. Arms, mouth, legs, all leaden. And he couldn't lift one small pinky.

"Pleasssse."

He had no concept of who heard his pleas, faint but persistent. A tattered hope where he had no understanding of what hope was. Maybe a muscle memory of what used to be.

He felt a twinkling of thought squeeze through the dark, a penlight of illumination. He clung to the raft, no longer adrift without mooring. Could he hold on to it?

"I am Junie."

The lab technician stood on rubber-soled shoes peering at the panel of numbers and graphs lighting up across the monitor's dashboard. He pulled a bottle labeled X724, plunged the syringe into it, and then released the liquid into the tubing connected to the IV bag that dripped into Junie's arm.

"If I could make a wager, this boy's facial expressions say he's fighting demons . . . and losing." He spoke in a monotone, detached, as he handed the needle to the nurse who held the medicine tray aloft. "Here, take it. As instructed, I need a new syringe for the next lab rat."

Her face stilled. "Lab rat? This poor baby is no rat. Watch yourself, Tech. Giving him this medicine should calm him down." She bent and made a note of the distortions Junie's face formed. "I do feel for all of them." Then smoothly, she pivoted, unzipped the plastic wall, and stepped through.

The tech followed her, zipping the wall closed behind him. He stood over the next bed and looked down at the feminine form lying as still as Sleeping Beauty and just as fair.

He ogled her and licked his lips. "Now, *she* seems to be having an entirely different dream experience."

Sinewy hands caressed her forearms and drew her near. Her eyes glided open, and she felt woozy, drunk on the need to feel this man's lips on hers. He seemed to be in a generous mood as his hand lifted to her face, cupping her chin, lifting bow-shaped lips to his, and then consuming her with wild abandon.

"How long?" her mind screamed.

A seductive roll of his shoulders positioned him to pull her body flush against his. "How long what?" he whispered into her ear, kissing its inner curve, sending waves of shivers across her body.

"Will I be stuck here? You visit me in my dreams. But we could never build a home together. Release me from this intoxication."

"This is your dream, Sari. Your want, your need. It is you that summoned me, you who fuels my days and burns through my nights.

We will be together. Hurdles and dogged delays be blasted; I won't wait much longer."

Sari felt a flush of steam travel through her body. A heated fog mist curled around the space that recently held her biggest temptation. He had vanished, replaced by a murky cloud that settled around her. She took a shallow breath and succumbed.

"My name is Sari."

Leaning forward, the nurse dabbed a cloth along Sari's forehead. "I think this medicine affects them all in slightly different ways. As soon as you put that new formula in her, she flushed red, sweating profusely."

Gliding past the once-again still form and through to the next transparent plastic wall to the last bed, Tech motioned for her to catch up. "Not my issue. Whatever this new formula is, they seem to be waking up after five months of hibernation."

Zipping the wall up behind her, she held out the loaded syringe. "Hibernation? They're not animals."

"Debatable. The brass calls each a perfect specimen, and I call them what they all are: animals. We work at the zoo, girl, and we're not even allowed to go home for some comfort. We're stuck here providing the feed and care of the residents."

"You are not a nice person. While we're getting paid in a short time what it would take us three years to earn, I'm thankful for the blessings. Let's take care of this gentleman and get off shift, shall we?"

John's throat felt brittle. His mouth was so parched that he dreamed he staggered through hot shifting sand, no water in sight. In this wilderness, he was never alone; two followed. And each time he looked back to tell the boy and girl who trailed behind him to keep up, he would find they were drowning in a whirlpool pit of sand. They floundered, and although he was desperate to reach them, they were sucked deeper into the widening hole before he could help. Frantically, he scrambled, falling on hands and knees, cut by grit as he feverishly dug. Suddenly, the wind would quiet, and the sand became snow. Screaming in noiseless terror, he succumbed and suffocated in the icy grave.

His dry throat and the nightmares looped on replay. He was in an eternal blurred reality. He desired something but didn't know what he wanted. He tried focusing on the two people in the dream with him. He felt a connection but didn't know why. His thoughts were elusive at the edge of nothingness. It was maddening. He hungered to fight his way through but couldn't lift his arms and punch himself free. He was held captive.

I'm so tired. Lord, hear my cry!

John's chest rapidly inflated in and out. His throat became Sahara dry again. He trudged through the sand, tasting grit on his tongue. The sequence had begun again, and he was powerless to stop it.

"My name is John."

The tech zipped close the protective plastic covering surrounding his last patient. Peeling off his gloves and dropping them on the tray, he reached up and keyed in his tasks for the last hour.

The nurse spun and laid her medicine tray in a bin labeled for collection and sanitization. "I'll be back later for their last therapeutic massage of the day. I'll see you tomorrow, Tech."

Their movements in synchronized symmetry, the two separated outside the clinic, moving in different directions. The lab tech headed to his room to catch the last of the basketball playoffs.

Her face now away from an audience, contorted at the gullibility of man, Dr. Carol Heathrow, known only to the staff as "Nurse," strode to report her latest findings.

Checking her surroundings, she knocked on the door, and hearing "enter," she looked around and sashayed into the room.

Edgar awaited her, his hands flat on the desk, pensive. "Talk to me. I need some good news."

"Calm down, honey. I have excellent news." She slinked around the desk and circled her arms around him from behind, draping her frame over his intimately, her front to his back. His wiry forearms strained, and his body caved into the desk as she seductively purred into his ear. "Have you been a good boy? Hmmm?"

Biting his bottom lip, voice trembling in a husky manner, he moaned, "Yesssss, I've been *very* good." Eyes icing with calculation, he shifted their positions, hoisted her onto the desk, and then lifted her scrub top over her head. "Talk to me."

"Formula X724 is working! After months of trial and error, your idea to blend the HeLa cells with your formula was the key. We are seeing facial expressions and ticks for the first time in five months."

"I thought it would work. I studied the miracle of HeLa cells many years ago in college. Can you believe the cells were only $250 a vial online? People forget, but when in doubt, go back to the basics." Tapping her hand in a rhythmic beat, he emphasized, "We can't blow this now. Three perfect human specimens. No sickness, cells pristine. No lungs filled with pollutants. No organs petrified by chemicals. No human bodies with metals leaking from crass orifices. We're going to be rich!"

"Richer."

"Tomato, tomato. Do you understand what one body of cells did for mankind? We will have three. Three! I will be wealthy beyond my dreams."

She cleared her throat. "Don't you mean *we'll* be wealthy?"

Grabbing her throat in his large hand, he roughly squeezed.

She breathed into his roughness like a fish to water. "Whatever you say, darling."

Stroking his chest, she glowed. "Now, you can leave that wife of yours and your little appetizer, the country bumpkin. *I'm* your main course, so feast, my love."

Laughing, he leisurely licked up the side of her face. "You must admit you enjoyed our little threesome, didn't you?"

Carol shrieked, "No, Edgar, that was for you." Then pushing his head away from her and sliding off the desk, she snatched her shirt back over her head. "Now, you've managed to piss me off and destroy the mood."

Laughing more, Edgar sat on his desk and folded his arms. "Listen, don't move too fast with their warming now that we have the key. The Boiler Room is not ready. The filtration systems need to come online first, then be flushed. After that, the engine and generators will follow, with the last being the air filters. We should be ready for habitation in three weeks. It's not easy to build what we're creating."

"God built the earth in six days. I wonder if hell is waiting for both of us? I get why we need their bodies, but why take them through torture first?"

"I'm not God, just godly. Your provincial religious upbringing is showing. It was cute before I had you in my bed, with my appetizer between your legs. Now it's just tiresome."

Tapping her foot, Carol said, "Meeting you, I've walked away from everything I've known as right and wrong. But you didn't answer my question. Why the cruelty?"

Tightening his tie with a smug look, he said, "Well, there are the crazies who are still privately pushing the notion of eugenics, and they're willing to pay me a boatload of money to prove them right. Allowing them to view tapes of this experiment is going to cost them plenty. So everywhere I look, I win." He then sat and pulled a large leather-bound book out of his drawer and onto his desk.

"Why such cruelty, Edgar?"

"Tsk-tsk, dear girl. Basically, it's because I can."

<h1 style="text-align:center">Chapter Fourteen</h1>

"It's been months, man," Bebop stressed. "If Edgar hadn't decided to allow us to go home because we proved ourselves loyal, I'd be out of a job or—"

"—dead!" Zachary finished for him. "I get it, but complaining won't give us more information. We know they are building something huge that none of us can get to."

Bebop added, "Listen, man, if we haven't found anything yet, maybe we never will. Nothing we've tried has worked."

"I got some undetectable surveillance equipment from one of our boys that should help. This software is so new that it should get by anything Edgar has in his office."

Bebop exhibited a grown-man pout. "You mean like the last equipment I had to flush down the toilet?"

"No, better than that, but just so you know, that was thousands of taxpayer dollars you flushed."

"Better it flushed," Bebop bemoaned, "than me."

Zachary's phone beeped. He pulled it out, glanced at it, and then turned toward the doorway. "I'm out. That's Edgar texting for an update, stat."

Bebop leaned back in his chair, and balancing on its two feet, he lifted his chin and fist-bumped Zachary. "Go do you. See you on the flip."

Striding out of the dorm room, Zachary lifted the peace sign in the air.

When he got to the hallway leading to Edgar's office, he saw it was lined with men who appeared to be someone's high-level security team.

I've been replaced?

A pit of cold in his stomach swirled as he knocked once and was told by Edgar to enter.

The room was as full inside as it was outside, and standing at attention was Edgar. Sitting in a leather wingback chair was the well-known media hound, Senator Jacob Benson. And standing behind his chair was none other than his old comrade, Legend.

Zachary had just become bipolar. He was happy and miserable all at once to see Legend. His friend had waded into the dark waters, and Zachary was nervous that seeing him meant the precarious tilting they had been doing for the last five months was about to be upended.

Legend blinked at him but showed no other signs of their past relationship. Following his lead, Zachary did the same.

Taking a giant step forward, Zachary stood at attention, "Sir. Senator. How can I be of service?"

Edgar peered at Zachary intently, conveying a message he wasn't sure he was interpreting correctly.

Edgar snipped, "The senator, our most esteemed benefactor, has apprised me of receiving word that things are going on in this building that I might not be aware of. I assured him that he had to be wrong. I employ top security—a past Special Forces officer—who'd let nothing get past him."

He now knew his role. Although loathed to play it, play it he did. "Yes, sir. There is nothing new to report. My men are on constant alert for anything that might harm the integrity of the labs or your stellar work, sir. Perhaps the senator can help me by describing what I should be looking out for."

Legend leaned forward and whispered into the senator's ear. The senator tapped his cane on the floor as though he had made a decision. He then spoke. "I am involved in many enterprises. Some bring me wealth, some bring me power, and some bring me hope for the future." He leaned forward on his cane and stared first at Edgar and then Zachary. "When I am fortunate, the hope for the future will bring me wealth *and* power."

He then grinned and settled back into his chair. "Approximately five and a half months ago, three Black bodies were recovered from my fracking site. Then without a 'kiss my raggedy asset'—'cause I know that must have been what you were saying to me—they were spirited away into the night."

Jumping to his feet, he slammed his cane across the desk, inches from Edgar's hands. "But I got my ways, by God. So imagine my surprise when one of the workers on the site finally was broken enough under Legend's wonderful tutelage to tell us he contacted you, Edgar . . . Which leads me here today."

The senator then delicately tucked his tie back into his jacket, which had fallen out when he struck the desk. Then running his hand through his hair, he quietly sat down.

No one dare stirred. It was mouse-pissing-on-cotton quiet.

Trembling, a puff of air escaped as Edgar stumbled over his words. "He's l-lying. There has been no nighttime scavenging of any bodies. How would I even know to do such a thing? You are one of my biggest contributors. I would *never* jeopardize our relationship."

Staring at him an uncomfortably long time, the senator drawled, "See, that's what I wondered too. Why would you have anyone on any of my sites reporting to *you*? Unless . . . You've been cheating me for years! A mineral here, an extraction there. And, bingo, you're getting paid at both ends."

The senator placed his cane upright and tapped the floor in emphasis. "Genius, really. I'd tip my hat to you . . . if it wasn't me you were ripping off."

Edgar's face paled, and sweat ran freely down each side of his cheeks. Swiping across the evidence of his fear with his handkerchief, he swallowed hard.

Awww, this here fool about to get all of us killed, Zachary thought, then cringed when the senator snapped his fingers. "Good. I take your silence as an agreement for Legend to take a look around." He waved his hands forward, and Legend moved stealthily to the door.

Edgar glared intensely at Zachary as he croaked, "See to it, man. Leave no stone unturned."

Zachary pivoted on his heels and turned. He marched out of the room with Legend on his flank. Being in Legend's presence brought back many memories, not all of which were good. Legend was prettier than handsome. There was a delicacy to his facial features, but none transferred to the man himself. Blond, blue-eyed, and over six foot three, he was as crazy and sly as a fox. Many had underestimated him . . . and lost. Now, Zachary was on his radar, which was never a good place to land. He needed to throw Legend's natural GPS into a tailspin, but how?

Shutting the door behind him, Legend grabbed Zachary from behind.

A mouth to his ear, Legend said softly, "I always thought one day I'd end up having to kill you."

Zachary stilled. "Get your hands off me before I have to let your mama know you finally wrote a check your butt couldn't cash."

Swiveling around, the men high-fived and hugged.

Legend then stepped back and surveyed him. Shaking his head, he slapped Zachary's six-pack stomach. "Too many fine meals with that fine wife of yours? Huh, man?"

Smirking, Zachary shook his head. "Nah, dude. I just got a life outside of drilling twenty-four-seven. Don't let this six-pack fool you. I can still get with you."

Holding his hands in the air as a sign of surrender, Legend gestured his head toward the closed door. "How did you end up doing slime duty?"

"When you have a fine wife, you do what is needed," Zachary said sarcastically.

"Honeymoon over?" Legend asked.

"Let's just say, some things are best experienced at a distance, and coming home brought certain things to light."

Tipping his head in acknowledgment, Legend turned to his men. "I'm going to do some recon. You men stay here." Then sweeping his arm out before him, he said, "Let's get this party started."

Zachary stepped in front of his old frenemy and wondered if this was how the rabbit felt when the fox cornered him.

Chapter Fifteen

Muscles tensed, face stoic, Zachary stood under the pounding torrent of water that flowed over him. He was exhausted. Everything about the day spelled future disaster in the making. Lying to his friend, stumbling over what he did there daily, he looked and sounded like a bumbling idiot.

Whatever Edgar was up to, the good senator smelled it, could taste it, and would soon devour them all. It was only a matter of time. And there was one thing Zachary understood about Legend . . . He never gave up.

Allowing the heat to ease his tension slowly, Zachary thought back to when they lost a terrorist they were tracking in Afghanistan. In defeat, Zachary had halted the hunt for the night. The men prepared to buckle down when Legend asked for the first watch. The men were grateful, but instead of waking halfway through the night for their watch, they awoke the next morning with the terrorist gagged and bound to a tree. He was barely alive, skin hanging loosely from various areas of his body. Legend must have half-carried or dragged him back to the campsite. And there Legend was, eating his rations with a deadly gleam in his eye, his knife stuck in the ground by his feet. He then calmly announced to the unit that he knew where the terrorists were making camp, and it was time to go hunting.

A towel now slung around his neck, Zachary opened the bathroom door to Sylvia lying on his bed.

"Right on time, honey." Inhaling deeply, she simpered, "You smell divine and look even better."

Quickly placing the towel around his waist, Zachary stopped. "Sylvia, I moved out of our room for a reason." Then going to the closet and taking out his robe, he slid into it. "To what do I owe this honor?"

Sylvia slid off the bed, her mouth in an unattractive moue, and slinked over to Zachary, stroking the lapels of his robe she attempted to open. But he caught her hands and removed them. "Uh, no, thank you. What can I do for you?"

"You can act like I'm your wife!"

"Now, that would mean that you weren't out in these streets acting as though you didn't have a husband."

Stomping over to the bed, Sylvia folded her arms in frustration. "You took my name off two of your bank accounts. How were you able to do it? I never signed to be taken off."

"Sure you did when you signed the papers to increase my life insurance. Unfortunately, you were so busy signing up for more money, you never read any of the papers you were signing."

"How could you, Zachary?"

"Originally, I did it because you were spending us into the poorhouse. I had to do something to slow you down. You still have access to the household bank account."

Screaming, Sylvia jumped up. "That's chicken scratch! I can't live off that."

"It's more than you made when you were working a nine to five. Woman, you are bleeding me dry. Those accounts were fat from my time in the military. Fat on my sweat, my pain, and yes, my fears. And you were spending it on pedicures!"

Advancing on him with a menacing look in her eye, she growled. "Give it back."

"No."

Pausing, a calculated gleam in her eye, she stepped out of her gown, caressing her body, then softly moaned, "I miss you, daddy. Forget the money. Come back to our room and let's make up the way we used to. I don't want to fight."

"No." Zachary moved her out of his way, and with his pants and shirt, went back into the bathroom, slamming the door behind him.

He heard her screech, and then a lamp and knickknacks hit the wall. "You come out here!"

Humming, Zachary put on his clothes to leave. He wasn't going to get any rest here tonight.

Thirty minutes later, Zachary arrived at the dorm room, hoping beyond hope that Bebop was present. He wasn't, but who he did find was Tom, anxious and pacing.

"Hey! What are you doing here?" Tom said as he rushed forward. "Doesn't matter. I was waiting on William, and then I was going to call you. They're moving the people down to the next level. All I could find out is they call the area the Boiler Room."

"Slow down. The Boiler Room? What's that?"

"I don't know, but there's a lab tech down there who has disappeared. Before he left, he asked to speak to me. He spoke so jumbled I couldn't get everything he was saying. But it was something about 'letting the animals free' and that 'a nurse wasn't a nurse,' and he was afraid for his life."

Zachary motioned up at the camera and then motioned for Tom to come closer. "Man, you yourself have helped on the monitors. How are you speaking in front of them?"

Tom smoothed his shirt down and took a deep breath. "Because I didn't sign up for this. Did you hear me say the tech is missing? He snuck off-site without permission to see his family and let it drop to the nurse that it was possible to sneak off. He then told her that his family couldn't believe what was happening at the facility, reviving Black folk. They sound suspiciously racist."

Rolling his eyes, Zachary roared in an undertone, "Can you stick to one topic? Who cares if they're racist? Tell me about this tech."

"He was waiting for me by my car when I got off yesterday. He liked to give me a heart attack, hunkered down as he was between a truck and my car. He was shaking and speaking so fast that he was hard to follow. He said he didn't think the nurse was a nurse. How the Boiler Room was ready, and the real experiments would begin. He then said that if they were reviving monkeys, the world as we knew it was doomed. He told his family because they were affiliated with people who could 'do something about it.'"

"Tom, this information should have been given to me posthaste."

"I couldn't. When I came back into the building, you were with Edgar. Then every time I saw you, you were with some Adonis-looking guy. I came here to tell William because I don't know if the tech compromised me. I *do* know he's missing."

"How do you know?"

"Because I wanted him to meet me in an hour, and he didn't show. I went looking for him, and none of his colleagues had seen him. When I asked the nurse about this, she hadn't seen him either."

"Maybe he went home."

"Negative. The front desk had several messages from his family stating they could not reach him, and he was not answering his cell phone. So you think he's dead?" Tom looked hard at Zachary. "Oh my God, you think he's dead, don't you? I didn't sign up for this!"

"Shush, man. What happened to hashtag team Zachary?"

Tom stopped pacing and gaped at Zachary in a panic. "Are you for real? I just wanted to help—not *die* from helping. Y'all don't even like me."

Yeah, and I'm disliking you more every minute you stand here whining.

"Man, go home. I'll look into this some more today. But do me one favor. Check in with your cousin and see if you can get back into Edgar's study."

"There was nothing there, man, and at this point, I'm not trying for my luck to run out."

"There was nothing there *then*. Since the senator's visit, everything may have been moved there for safekeeping. Just one more time, man, can you do it? For your cousin?"

Exhaling, Tom nodded his head. "One more time, and that's it. If that tech is dead, then we're all in danger. Maybe stopping this is the only way for us to get out alive."

Zachary patted Tom's back in agreement. He couldn't open his mouth and lie and tell him that they were all in great danger now that Legend was on the scent of trouble.

Zachary skirted the cameras and lay down on the bunk. Thinking hard, he waited for Bebop. The last thing he instructed Tom to do before he left was to show an empty dorm with empty bunks on the monitor, but a man couldn't be too careful. Settling in, he waited for Bebop. Now, only one other guard was working twelve-hour shifts, so Bebop had to be on his way. The other guards worked the outer parameter.

Bebop limped into the dorm—his past injury noticeable in his despair—like a man in a trance. When he looked up at Zachary, there were tears in his eyes. He opened his mouth and then closed it. Sitting down on the closest chair, he sighed and then wiped his eyes.

"How long have you known me?" Bebop asked.

"Huh, what?"

Bebop's voice resonated with a sorrow so distinct that Zachary sat at attention. "We've fought terrorists. We've seen small children used as weapons of warfare. We've witnessed little old ladies pushing baby buggies full of explosives. But I've never—"

"Never what, man?"

"Felt every millimeter of the melanin in my skin covering every part of my body."

"I don't understand."

His voice was so faint that Zachary had to lean forward to hear Bebop speak. "I was called to move the three people to a special area called the Boiler Room. I don't think they wanted to use me, but for some reason, the tech was missing, and it was like some nurse had made a split-second decision. So I get in the freight elevator with all three bodies on rolling gurneys. We barely fit in there. This nurse, she takes out a special key and plugs it into the keypad on the wall, and we go past the basement and on the top, where the floors light up after the basement, it's just blank, but we're still moving down."

"Down? Below even the area where they had us where the clinic was held?"

"Down—where hell meets your soul, and you're never the same."

"Darn. Bro, go on."

"Well, I get out and . . . wow, get this . . . there's grass and shacks like back in slavery time. There's a horse by a trough, drinking. And if you look off, it looks like there's nothing but miles and miles of land. And get this, *slaves are working in the fields.* But how can that be?"

"I don't get it."

"It's like the 1800s, man, and slavery has never ended. The nurse made me take them to a shack with old dusty pallets of straw on the floor and had me leave them there. When the sheets came off them, they were dressed like *slaves!*"

"No!!!"

"And we've stepped right in it! Whatever this is, it's the most demonic thing I've ever seen. I think they are going to treat those people like slaves. Man, is this a movie I need to wake up from?"

"I don't know. But I'm worried about you. No way is Edgar going to allow you to leave or tell anyone what you saw. So the only way to protect you is to act as though what you saw did not bother you."

"Bother me? Man, I'm gutted."

Zachary stared off and stated, "Better you *feel* gutted than *be* gutted."

As they spoke, they could hear footsteps in the hallway. Zachary ducked into the shower. Using his new remote transmitter, he took the empty bunks off the monitor. Hearing voices outside as they got closer, he heard Edgar state he had to be in the dorms.

Swinging the door open where it bounced into the wall behind it with a resounding bang, Edgar made his grand entrance. Directly behind him was the woman they called Nurse. Directly behind her was Marilyn.

"Ah, there you are. I'll have to have someone check the monitors. For some reason, we couldn't see you in here."

Standing at attention, Bebop answered, "I just stepped in, sir."

"Let me introduce you to Dr. Carol Heathrow, who we fondly call 'Nurse.' Unfortunately, she had a bit of trouble as a doctor, and they removed her credentials. But we both know that knowledge learned can't be taken away from you, can it, Bill?"

"Uh, no, sir."

"In that same way, what you see becomes knowledge that can't be taken away from you. Are you following me?"

Zachary could hear Bebop's deep swallow. "Yes, sir. I'm following you."

"Are you a betting man, Bill?"

"No. I like . . . sure things," Bebop answered in a hesitant voice.

"Well, isn't it your lucky day? I'm sure you will be dead this time tomorrow and your wife a widow if you give me any problems."

Bebop stood at attention. Zachary could see his left leg tensing.

Don't do it, man; don't fight them, Zachary thought, hoping he had suddenly been emboldened with telepathic powers.

Marilyn stepped forward and whipped out her Glock. "Enough talk. Kill him now, dump him with the tech, and make it appear as though they fought each other. Didn't you say the tech was from a well-known, right-wing family?"

Edgar cleared his throat. "Just because he was from a right-wing family that spouted conspiracy theories doesn't mean everything you tell them, they'll buy."

Marilyn snorted. "A Black man and white man have words, the nurse here overhears. Later, she witnesses the Black man threatening the white man. Then they're both found in the abandoned gas station up the street where they've shot each other. This is the tech's Glock. I found it in his glove compartment."

Rubbing his chin, Edgar thought for a while. He then hunched his shoulders and said, "Or we can use him in our experiment. And if he gives us any problems, kill him then."

Dr. Heathrow finally spoke up. "I like that better. You'll be able to research the art of betrayal. How does it feel to do what so many did in those days . . . betray your own? You know there would have been no slavery if they had stuck together and not turned on each other and sold their own. I read that some Black people actually owned slaves."

Chortling, Edgar pounded his hands together. "Talking about Black-on-Black crime, this gets better and better. As a matter of fact, I'm feeling so good about it, I want to celebrate." Then turning to Carol, he crowed,

"Call the country bumpkin, darling. I think it's time for another stroll down memory lane."

"No! I'm *not* dealing with that stupid cow. You promised, Edgar. A one and done. What do you see in her anyway?" Carol asked.

"Her greed matches mine. She got right down on her knees when I first met her for me to give her husband the head of security job here. When I saw his credentials, I would have hired him without her added incentive. I knew then anything I asked she would do—unlike *you*, Carol."

"Unlike *me*?" she screeched. "You caused me to lose my physician's license, then put me on this project where my tech assistant winds up dead. I think I've done more for you than a hump and bump."

Marilyn grabbed Bebop's arm. "Enough talk about your tawdry sex life, Edgar. This is why we aren't together anymore. You always get sidetracked by the mundane. It's your weakness, and one day, it will be your downfall."

Edgar's smile was so sinister that Marilyn visibly quivered. "And the day that happens," he said, "hope that you're far, far away."

Her gun trained on Bebop, she pushed him out of the room, and the others followed.

Hearing their steps recede down the hall, Zachary released a long breath. When Sylvia's role in his hiring came up, so did his lunch from earlier. There he stood with vomit in his hand while he tried not to run out there and kill them all. He should have never left home without his gun. He could have at least gone to his office and picked one up. But Sylvia angered him so much that he left as quickly as possible and headed straight to the dorm room.

Now, Bebop was in custody as some kind of tool in a strange experiment. People were being held as though slavery still existed, Legend hot on all their tails, and Sylvia was in an affair with his boss. When you added up everything going on in his life, you could totally say he was royally screwed.

Maybe, Bebop was right. He did need Jesus.

Chapter Sixteen

Junie battled to open his eyes, but the glue was stuck to his eyelids, and the gravel someone had placed there was gritty and felt like fire when he attempted to lift his lids. Finally, using his forefinger, he gently pried them open. Due to the rapid beating of his heart, peeking was against his better judgment, but he had to see what was happening. The last thing he remembered was a wall of white turned to black, excruciatingly cold turned to pain, and then . . . nothing.

He was on a pallet on the floor. Under his pallet was packed dirt. His clothes were shredded, but the material was not scratchy like his everyday clothing. Instead, it was soft and worn. And they fit. He looked at his hands. They were clean, although his fingernails remained dirty. Touching his hair, he found it in long strandlike ropes. His chest moved rapidly as panic began to set in.

"Easy now, son. Easy."

"Papa? Papa?" Junie cried as he crawled to his knees.

Junie looked over and saw his father sitting near him with his sister's head in his lap. "You a'ight, son?"

"Don't know. My eyes hurt sometin' fierce and my legs weak as a newborn foal. I reckon my head won't fall off but surely feel like it."

"Sounds 'bout right. Same tin happened to me. Dere's some water in a basin over in de corner. Splash your'n eyes til dey betta," John said, stroking Sari's hair and rocking her in his arms.

Junie stumbled a little as he stood but wobbled his way to the water on a small table in the corner. He poured the tin pitcher into the basin and flushed his eyes until he no longer felt the grit.

"Papa, how longs I been sleepin'?"

"I don't rightly know, Junie. I woke a bit ago, den you'se. Now, we wait on Sari."

"What you member last? Is dis c'here Colorado?"

John gently laid Sari down, stood, and hugged his young son to him hard and fast. "Junie, I'se know no mo' den you. Looks like we been caught like a piglet in a snare, but where de owl? And, is our enemy as wise?"

Junie sat down and closed his eyes. Where was the voice of Heaven? Where was the word that came right on time? He said go, and they went. What was the reward for their obedience?

Tears ran down Junie's face. "I can't hear nothin', Papa." Junie grabbed his father around the waist. "What we gon' do?"

"We gon' wait on it."

Both John and Junie Benson turned around to see Sari work her way to sit up on her pallet. She blinked rapidly as Junie ran and brought the basin with clean water to her. "Flush your eyes, Sari girl. Keep on till dey clear of de grit."

Sari did as she was told and soon opened her eyes to her father and brother. "We together! Dats sometin'."

Helping her up to her feet, John placed his arms around both of his children. "Right now, dis enough. We need to rest dese bodies, and den we need to figure out what's goin' on. Sometin' don't feel right c'here. What you member?"

Sari rose, slow but sure. "I had such joy in my heart—den *boom!* White came over—"

Sari stopped, eyes glazed with tears. She hugged herself and hung her head.

A large, calloused hand tenderly rubbed up and down on her arm. "I'se here, child. Papa is right c'here."

"—me. It covered my eyes, den my nose, den more cold den my bones ever felt, den dark, den nothing but my dreams."

Junie grunted. "Mo' like nightmares. Chasing, always chasing me—"

"And de dreams neva stop. Like a circle, dey was neva endin'," John whispered. He then shivered but braced his legs and exhaled. "We didn't come to dis place on our own. So, sometin' very right or wrong don' found us. We wait to see which way de wind blow."

Junie nodded, feeling the same as his father. Whatever was happening, they were together, and he would pray with all that was within him that His voice would return.

Later, when his stomach warned him it was past the time to eat, Junie felt his arm throbbing. Looking down, he saw pin-sized puncture holes in his inner arm. Examining more of his body, he saw similar holes in his other arm. Sitting up, he pushed on his father's shoulder and woke him.

"Papa, what you reckon dis is?" Junie asked as he held out his arms and showed his father his tiny pricks.

"We's all got dem. I checked. My arm was sore, so I looked; didn't say nothin' 'cause don't wan't my worry to be your worry."

"But, Papa, we always share."

"Yeah, but I neva liked it. I'm da daddy who shoulda been makin' a way. Not lettin' you lead."

Junie looked at his father with a new set of eyes. "Papa! You neva let me lead. You let da voice lead. You said Heaven called, and we needed to heed dat good word. You don't no mo', Papa?"

John straightened his shoulders. "Yes, I's believe. Don't ya listen to my old man rumblings. I'se got mice in my head runnin' around. Can't catch them for dey run away with me mouth."

Sari stood, dusting off her dress. "Den better get dat cat after dat dere tongue, Papa."

Junie laughed. "Sari girl, look like instead of the cat having yo' tongue, it don' loosed yo' brain. You're right dere smart in dis here captivity."

Junie gasped as he uttered the dreaded word, *captivity*, and brought to light what none of them had wanted to say in the dark.

Had they run so far—only to be slaves again?

Earlier, John had pulled on the cabin door while the others slept and found it was locked. Later, Junie had tiptoed to the door accompanied by his father's snores and pulled on it, but it kept its secrets on the other side. Finally, with one eye open, Sari saw both her papa's and brother's futile attempts, squeezed her eyes, and prayed very hard for a way out. She still believed in the voice that sent them scurrying into the Christmas night, that the God she knew would come.

Hours passed, the door creaked open, and a man appeared. He looked ill at ease in his clothing, the material which seemed too rough and hewn to the touch as he tugged and squirmed with each precision step. Ironically, Junie felt he resembled their old overseer, ruddy-faced with grizzled cheeks and thin lips. The difference lay in his eyes that bespoke cunning intelligence and his constant squint, as though in need of spectacles.

"You!" he barked in a thin, reedy voice, pointing to John. "Come with me, now."

Used to obeying orders from those who looked like the man in front of him, John moved as though by rote. Nodding to Junie and Sari to be still, Junie could tell he was anxious to go and find out who or what held them.

Junie's acquired skill at eavesdropping wouldn't work here all locked away. So all he could do was pray. Pray for intervention. If he was right, even without the voice guiding him, he had enough sense to know it wouldn't be long before they came for him and Sari.

"They comin' for us next, huh, Junie?"

Eyes narrowed, Junie studied Sari. "Well, knock me back a time or two, Sari girl. You don' hit yo' head and come out right side up."

Sari huffed and leaned against the wall. "You know, Junie Benson, when a person acts a certain way, nothing much is expected of them." She twirled around and screeched out real high, "I declare, Junie, it's just too much; yes, it is."

Mouth open wide, Junie scratched his head. Sari laughed out loud. "You don't know if you should scratch your head or pat your bottom."

"We family, Sari. Why ya play us dumb?"

"Because you thought I was. You and Papa, plotting and carrying on, all the while keeping me protected . . . from me. Let me tell you something. I was under the missus day in and day out, and I could talk like her, walk like her, and out-think her. So, who's the pet, Junie?"

Junie stumbled down onto his pallet. He marveled at his sister, then stood and did a jig. " Sis, you slicker den a greased pig!" he crowed, laughingly falling back into the dirt.

"I'm too worn out from it all, Junie," she said. Sari flopped down next to him, looking sober. "Look at this." She grabbed the one tin cup lying near his bed. She turned it sideways and used it as a tool as she scraped for several minutes, removing the dirt into a small mound until they could see a glimmer of a hard floor. "What's this?"

Scampering onto his knees, Junie looked at the floor. He took the cup and began to bore a wider hole in the dirt. They knocked on the floor and felt its solid surface when he got about a foot down.

"It's sho' 'nough solid." Junie marveled at it. He spat down into the hole and rubbed it. He tried to scratch in it, but it resisted. "I don't know. But we betta cover it back up, den later, let Papa see it."

"*If* he comes back," Sari said as she pressed her and Junie's foreheads together. "Time you let me be the big sister, Junie. I gon' protect you."

Junie hugged her back and proclaimed, "You protect me? I'm gon' hav' to sit on the new Sari for a while. It's a thang to behold."

"Think on this, Junie. I was with Missus more than anyone else after Mama died. And Mama never wanted anybody to know that I wasn't dim. She said that the combination of how I looked was a danger to me and a threat to them. My life be easier than hers if I keep myself to myself from everyone. Like to kill me some days, play-acting."

Junie hunched his shoulder in protest. "Seem to me ya got real good at it. Real good. Darn near wanting to choke you some days good, Sari."

"Never mind. What you think, Junie? And I'll be sharing this with Papa myself, you hear me?"

Hearing the door open, they jumped apart. As Sari sat on top of the newly discovered floor, the same man from earlier now pointed to Junie.

"You, come with me."

Junie stood and squeezed his sister's shoulder as he left the small shack. Walking outside, he looked up at the sky and felt the glare from the sun on his face, then observed the horse at the trough. Junie stared hard, trying to see what felt off about the whole thing. Then inhaling, he reached for the assurance that just because the voice was silent didn't mean no one was there. And although he was stepping into the unknown, he was not alone.

A hard shove up the stairs of a small wooden porch had him look closely at where he was. He calculated that this would have been the dreaded overseer's residence if he was home. The door opened into the living room. Two men sat behind a desk similar to the one Massa Benson would do his business at in the past. Both men resembled in dress his old Massa, but one smelled exceptionally good. Junie had never come across a man who smelled so pleasant. Where was the smell of tobacco, horseflesh, and the sweat of the fields?

Leaning into the delightful aroma, Junie was grabbed from behind and snatched into the hardback chair. Looking down, he saw minuscule droplets of blood on the floor. Pensive, he understood if there was blood, Papa hadn't easily told them what they wanted to know. He would also need to be wise in what he said to them.

"All right, boy, what's your name?" the man who smelled so good asked.

"Junie, suh, and yours?"

Looking at the other man, the man smirked. "*I'm* the one who asks the questions. This is the Burstein Plantation, and you are now my property." He then stood in front of Junie. "What year is it, boy?"

"It's 1859. No, it's 1860, seeing as we were on the road for about a month. Yes'm, I say it's 1860."

The man, Edgar, looked giddy to Junie. He bounced around and slapped his hand on his knee. He turned to the other man and said excitedly, "Just as the artifacts spoke to, 1859 to 1860. My God, man! Pre-Civil War!"

The other man rushed out of the room in jubilation. Hearing the door slam, Edgar leaned forward. "Tell me how you did it."

"Did what?" Junie said.

"How'd you get here from there."

"Not rightly sho. We comin' up on Colorado, and then it was all white, then all black. Then we woke up here in dis c'here place."

Edgar paced back and forth, mumbling to himself. Junie sat and watched as the man stopped, began to speak, then shook his head and walked some more. Then as though he made a decision, he turned to Junie.

"Who's your massa, boy?"

Puzzled but defiant, Junie said, "You just said you were. But I say no one! We came to Colorado free. We gon' stay free."

A gleam in his eye, Edgar stated, "It is 1860, and you and your family are *not* free. But if you mind your manners, you will be taken care of as your people have always been taken care of in the past."

Walking over to Junie, he pulled up Junie's shirt. "Your skin does not bear any whipping marks, and that tells me you and your father are an obedient lot. I wonder what would make you runners."

Junie folded his arms. He was done talking. He knew enough to know when you gave out more information than you learned, it was time to be quiet.

"You gon' quiet on me? That's okay. Your father did too. But you'll talk when we're ready to hear more. Especially when we're ready to talk to that pretty sister of yours."

"You leave my sister alone!" Junie yelled.

"See how easy it is to get you to talk, boy?" Edgar rubbed his hands together as though he couldn't take the anticipation. "Your life, my boy, has just become priceless. Or maybe your death. It's your choice which."

Chapter Seventeen

A door abruptly banged open, and the man who had raced out of the room earlier stomped in and yanked Junie from the chair. He dragged him outside, while behind him, Edgar Burstein gleefully howled. Across the open yard, he pulled Junie, his arm feeling numb from the tightness of his grip. As they rounded a corner, there was his father, sledgehammer in hand, breaking a pile of rocks. Standing near him was a Negro man, dressed similarly to them, holding a bullwhip in his hands.

"Another one for you, Smith. Boss says see to it that he gets to work too. He wants these rocks broke by the end of the day."

The man's gaze held the white man's with a feral glint as his answer was a tilt of understanding, and the large white man, cheeks splotched, stormed away as though his feet were on fire.

Picking the sledgehammer off the ground, Junie went over to the rocks and began to hit them.

"Young son, do not look at me as I speak to you. Keep hitting those rocks in front of you—my name's Bill. You can call me Bebop when we are alone. I don't have much time, and you should know we're being watched. I understand from your father that you're a very bright person. I plan to help you get out of here after I figure out how I will get myself out of here. I think I can at least offer you hope that you're not alone."

Junie stopped to look at him when John said, "Keep workin', Junie. We being watched, and dis c'here man say he wit' us. We gon' see."

John turned, and Junie could finally see his entire face. He had a busted lip and an eye that was starting to bruise.

"Papa, dey hurt ya? I'se sorry, Papa."

"Boy, dey ain't don' nothin'. My head harder den' dey blows. I'se worried 'bout Sari. No tellin' how she gon' take all dis."

"Uh, Papa. Sari gon' be just fine." Junie grunted out of breath as he broke another rock. "She been playing possum in a nest of hornets, and she got more right thinkin' den we know."

John almost stopped working to puzzle out Junie's words. He then grinned wide. "Dat be ya mama's way. Neva let the right hand know what da left hand gon' do. She always said she hated dat dey knew her for smart, 'cause her smart pixie dusted Massa. Smart can get folk like us killed; ya mama knowed it."

"But dey knew I was smart, Papa."

"And Benson used it against us. But long as you had the voice, I wasn't worried 'bout ya. Ya had His protection."

"Benson? Senator Benson?" Bebop said.

"Don't know nothin' 'bout no senator. Mr. Jacob Benson of Benson Plantation, Tennessee, who'm talkin' 'bout. He was our massa. Now, he just a man who kept me a slave."

"Dang it, man. This can't be real. They said to pretend we were in 1860, and I figured you all had some collective amnesia, or they were doing some bizarre medical experiment. You trying to tell me y'all teleported in some kind of time machine to this time?"

Junie turned, and John said hurriedly, "You don' forget dey watchin', Junie?"

Bill made his face calm and said with his mouth barely moving, "Talk to me."

Junie bent low, picked up a rock he broke, and threw it in a nearby pile. "I'm Junie Benson. Dats my pa, John. My sister, Sari, is hopefully okay. We left her in the cabin." Junie wiped his forehead and slung the sledgehammer down. "We runaways. Made it all the way to Colorado. Fought thieves, animals, de weather. . .all to get there and be caught under the biggest blanket of snow we eva saw."

John then took over the story, their collective hammering of rocks providing a rhythm to its telling. "We woke up in de cabin, only to be told by Mr. Smell Good we still bound—"

"—He did smell good, didn't he, Papa? Neva smelled nothin' like it."

"Keep ya mind straight, Junie. But ya right. Smelled like a clean river flowin' into a waterfall. Don't know how he did dat." Clearing his throat, John continued, "I hope you be true to what ya say, Mister Bebop. Come too far to stop."

Talking ceased, and just the taps and pounding of rocks breaking could be heard.

"Please don't react to what I'm about to tell you. I'm still adjusting to the fact that you guys are one hundred sixty-three years in the future. At least I've seen science fiction movies. So how do I explain it to you? Guys, it's the year 2023. There is no slavery. Although we are still not where we should be as a people, technically, we're free."

"I don't understand, tech . . . ni . . . cally we're free." Junie sounded out. "We're free or no? It don't make sense."

"Junie, I think de man is tryin' to tell us in dis c'here time, we be loosed, but we still fightin' for dem to ack like it. Like free folk in our time, it be little free."

"Well said," Bill murmured.

"I don't want to be a little free. Papa be smart. Mama be smart. Den dey make me, and I'se real smart. But His voice be my compass, and without it, I feel lost. I feel lost, Papa!"

"What is this voice you speak of?" Bill said.

"Junie been gifted. He hear, and we do. But since he woke up, voice not speakin' and dat worries all of us. Da voice always know what to do."

"Jesus!" Bill said. "You're prophetic?"

"No diseases here, mister. I hear from Heaven, and I do what Heaven say do," Junie said. "He say leave, run on Christmas Day. And Christmas Day, we run."

Bill's eyes filled, and a tear crested his cheek. "I thought God had forsaken me. Left me here to die and burdened my heart with the evil

I've witnessed in the last several days. But my Father, who art in Heaven, has placed me here on purpose. One that is greater than my time as a Special Forces operative."

John hit the next rock so hard that Junie had to duck. "Don't rightly know what kind of forces you got so special dere, suh. But hope it help us get a plan, and we git gon'."

"Right, uh, let's see. I was in the army and was given skilled training for hard tasks. The more impossible the problem seemed, the more likely we were called in to fix it." Bebop looked over their heads as he said solemnly, "It seems my sworn oath is still needed. It won't be easy. But I understand my assignment."

John gave a derisive cackle Junie had never before heard from his father. "We ain't neva known easy. Me and mine built for hard."

Junie did as his father did and split the next rock so hard that the small pieces were too tiny to gather. Looking out to the sky and the sun that never seemed to warm his skin, he said, "Whateva dis place be, God has forsaken it but not us. He sent you, Mr. Bebop, until I could hear from him again."

"I hear you, son," Bebop said.

Junie bit his bottom lip and asked, "Mr. Bebop, suh. You talk real good. If we run, we gon' need to blend in. Can you help us do betta? Specially Papa?"

Rolling his eyes, John said, "You think I can't talk right if I try, Junie?"

"Well, I think we all need to practice like I did my letters. When we run, we can't stand out, Papa. Gon' be hard enough in this brand-new world."

John opened his mouth, and Junie interrupted. "I know, Papa. We built for hard. Just wish soft would give us half a chance."

Chapter Eighteen

Zachary left the bank smiling with the money he had withdrawn from every account in a cashier's check in his pocket. He left only a few hundred dollars in Sylvia's household account, and even that tiny amount made him cringe. After everything he had learned hiding in the dorm shower, he spent the next two days strategizing how to get word to Bebop, and Bebop get word to him. He also needed to make a beeline for Bebop's wife and children and move them to an undisclosed location. In dealing with a maniac, your flank is the one thing you better cover. Bebop's weakness was his wife and son, and Edgar would move on them as prey. Then when Edgar tries to find Bebop's family, he wouldn't, and if by chance he did find them, he'd be running into a group of men so feral that Edgar Burstein and any he sent wouldn't survive.

There was a campground made up of ex-Special Force members, primarily those who suffered physically or mentally for their country . . . A country that failed to treat them as the heroes they were, especially since some of their most significant victories were top-secret missions.

Zachary had been secretly affiliated with them since his return stateside. Their program on investing the finances of strapped veterans had many of the men solvent for the first time since joining the service. Three of their members took them into cryptocurrencies before the media even understood what the metaverse was, and they all had prospered. Zachary had never let Sylvia know any of this, but she spent like he had sat down and given her clearance to act a fool with his life savings. He called for help when Bebop was taken. The guys were happy to come in and get Bebop's family. They were even willing to pick up Bebop's mother-in-law. Mother Sweat was a paragon of virtue and wisdom. And she made the best collard greens and pound cake he had ever tasted in his life. She was the one that told him that a pair of green eyes don't make a marriage and "*Never Trust a Big Butt and a Smile*" that could lure him into regretting his haste. He foolishly thought she was talking out of her head—this elderly woman quoting Bell Biv DeVoe. Instead, he now understood that she knew what he hadn't. She was a godly woman, and since he and God hadn't seen eye to eye since he had been in the armed forces, he blocked out any "religious" speak he heard from her. And she and the rest of Bebop's family were Bible-thumpers.

Pulling into his driveway, he scowled. Sylvia was home, and fury coursed through his veins. He wanted to choke the evil out of her and reverse the fact they ever met. Could he navigate the next several days with her and keep Edgar and Legend unaware? Because with everything else going on, Zachary was sure that Legend had him followed because he would do the same. So he had to razzle-dazzle his tail, get Bebop's family to safety, and pull off, helping this enslaved family and Bebop escape without leaving a trail. He would need some hocus-pocus and razmataz.

He gave a full belly laugh, thinking of his clandestine meeting with Bebop's family as they pulled off to their safe house. He knew his friend would want to see that he personally saw them off to safety. The last to get into the car, Mother Sweat pulled him into her ample bosom and breathed, "Confucius say the person who chases two rabbits catches none."

The woman was an anomaly, quoting Confucius and Bell Biv DeVoe. He guessed her words would ring true when needed, and Zachary welcomed the release of laughter he had going home. Then resolve settled heavily in his stomach as he pulled onto his street. Once home, he stopped laughing. He hated feeling like he was a quitter, but he knew he would not regret breaking the ties he hastily formed with Sylvia. Instead, he would regret that they had hurt each other far longer than they should have by trying to hold on. Then maybe when he made room for the actual green-eyed goddess, she would appear outside his dreams.

Putting his key in the door, it refused to turn. He tried it again … and nothing. Finally, he banged on the door, yelling, "Sylvia, open this door."

Instead, the garage door opened, and he saw his belongings in overflowing garbage bags and haphazardly packed boxes.

Sylvia then proclaimed through the Ring camera, "You don't pay; you can't stay. You know I don't do romance without finance. You'll hear from my attorney. Be prepared to give me back everything you took from me."

"Thank you, Sylvia. Thank you," he screamed at the top of his lungs, making his nosy neighbor come to her door. Then rolling his eyes, he said, "Hello, Mrs. Jones. *Goodbye*, Mrs. Jones."

Retired, Mrs. Jones stepped out on her porch, placed her hand on her hip, and yelled over. "Since you want to be nasty, let me tell your deluded butt something. Your front door is more active between the hours of nine and six than a Macy's Day after Christmas Final Sale. And your misses is right patriotic the way she entertains the army, navy, and marines. USO ain't got nothing on her." Putting her fingers in a V-shape, she swung her fingers from her eyes to his house. Then with her paisley muumuu swishing around her stout legs, she stepped back inside and slammed the door.

Grunting while throwing his stuff into his trunk and backseat, a red flush of humiliation spread up his neck and across his face. *So this woman had the nerve to bring other men to my home? Edgar wasn't the* only *one?*

Marching back in front of the camera, Zachary yelled, "Thank you again, Sylvia. May you choke on your greed."

He heard the distinct click of the audio on Ring activate, then, "You're welcome. And every time I sip Champagne and munch on caviar, I'll think of you."

See, this woman is as dumb as rocks. Here she is allergic to seafood, and she'll eat caviar? I guess she will *choke on her greed. Dear Mother Sweat, does this make* me *prophetic?*

Humming with a newfound sense of relief, Zachary got into his car and pulled into traffic. Then hitting his phone option on his steering wheel, he called his attorney.

He spurted his need without the benefit of a "good day" when Stephen picked up. "Get it all rolling. I'm sending you Ring tapes of all the men Sylvia had in my home while I was bringing home the bacon, and she wouldn't even fry it in the pan."

"You're kidding," Stephen said.

"Courtesy of a nosy neighbor. It's obvious I didn't marry her for her intelligence."

"Guy, I'm sorry this happened to you. But I'll start the paperwork right away."

"Thank you. One more thing. Remember when I got your cousin the position in housekeeping at my job?"

"Oh, man, she's not messing up, is she? She told me she had gotten a promotion and was now over janitorial services, and it came with a nice bonus."

"She's good. I need to meet with her, but no one, and I mean *no one*, can know we are meeting. Can you arrange it?"

"Yeah, I can. You can meet Saundra at my aunt's home. She lives in a senior citizen village, and my cousin visits her at least twice weekly. So anyone who knows her won't think it's strange for her to go there. But, man, this is my fam, so don't make me regret the invite."

"You know I would never do you like that, bros, for life. And, man, the meet needs to be soon, as in yesterday."

"Hooah!" Stephen said.

Zachary left his new residence at a long-term motel and went directly to Independence Senior Village. When he checked in at the front desk, he gave the name Stephen had texted to him. The pleasant receptionist directed him to the apartment. Walking all the corridors thinking of his plan, Zachary wished he could believe in God because this would have been an appropriate time to say a prayer.

Knocking on the door, a jumpy Saundra answered and ushered him inside. "Mr. Trumble, my cousin said you needed to speak to me, and I needed to listen."

Zachary took in her apple cheeks, golden brown braids falling over her shoulders, and the question in her dark brown eyes and trembling of her clenched hands.

"I need you to brace yourself. What I'm going to share will not be easy or believable."

Saundra glowered. "Are you going to tell me about the plantation built on the floor that shouldn't exist at Burstein Labs?"

"What? How'd you—"

"—I made myself the best supervisor I could be and built a network of staff that don't see me as the enemy but as an ally. Mr. Burstein handpicked Saul. He's always been a stickler for the company's policies, and he cleans Mr. Burstein's private office area." Shuddering, Saundra continued, "When he got the assignment to collect the trash placed at the elevator behind a cluster of trees and bushes—*inside* our building—he was intrigued and investigated. Saul got down on his knees, crawled around the cluster of bushes, and saw a world that dated back over a hundred and fifty years."

"Talk to me. I have a friend I got into this mess, and I need you to get word to him. I need to figure out a way to stop this madness."

"Thank God!"

God, again? What is everyone drinking? Zachary ground his teeth and blinked. "Well, okay then. It sounds like you're on board. Tell me the rest of it."

"Saul's Jewish and his grandparents told him about the horrors of the Holocaust from when he was a small child. Seeing what he saw, he had a nightmare. So he came to see me last night, and then my cousin called and asked me to meet you."

Shaking her head as though she was still in disbelief, she said, "Saul saw several Black people; one had a whip and watched the other two, a boy and man, break rocks with a sledgehammer. They dressed as if the pages of a history book had shaken them out. He said he thought he would see cotton fields growing behind them. It was so vivid. And get this, there was even a horse grazing. Then before crawling back to the elevator, two white men he had never seen before came out of a cabin and stood talking. That's when he scrambled out of there."

"And people think there is a God? Son of a—"

"—I take it you aren't a believer, young man. But please, refrain from cursing in my home."

Turning, Zachary saw a tiny woman with coiffed silver hair in a pink pantsuit. Her makeup was artfully applied, and her manicured nails shined with a pearl polish. Marriage to Sylvia had trained him in such details, but she and Sylvia differed because she exuded Southern gentility under a steel magnolia mantle of strength.

"My apologies, ma'am. Your daughter just shared some disturbing news."

"I am aware," she said as they watched her move gracefully around her kitchen. She picked up a tray of cups and a teapot and returned to the living room. "Let me introduce myself. I'm Rose Wiley. When I was a teenager, I marched with my parents and Martin Luther King Jr. Such high hopes we all had. Then I saw strange fruit not falling from trees but police officers' bullets lying uncovered on the ground. Video recordings and eyewitness accounts failed to garner justice. Then we got a Black president of the United States of America. I felt hope *again*. At the end of his eight years, in utter disillusionment, we faced four years of backlash from folk so scared of equality that they have pushed us back sixty years."

Her small chest rose up and down as she shuddered, pouring the tea into teacups. "Saundra came to me this morning sharing all that had happened. Young man, if she did nothing, she would wither away in self-loathing. I raised her better; no job will take away her ability to do right in a world of wrong. So, Mr. Zachary Trumble, ex-Special Forces, how can we help?"

Zachary stood with a smile that had widened with every punctuation of Rose's fiery monologue. Injustice could make the most benign person have malignant intent. He wanted to fry someone, but the fire had to be tended carefully.

"Saundra, I need you to get Saul to get a message to Bebop."

"Bebop?"

"Bill, my inside man. Knowing Edgar, everything outside of that elevator is under surveillance. And I only say that because Saul would be dead now if they were watching that area. It also means Saul will need to be cagey. Do you think he can try to be there waiting when the next person places the trash and laundry there?"

"He knows the pickup schedule. So I would think that he could get there early and wait. But how will he get your message to this Bebop?"

"If dirty clothes go out, then laundered clothes must go in. We'll seal the note in the overseer's clothing. If I know one thing, Bebop is meticulously clean, almost OCD, and he will not see the other guards get fresh and clean changes of clothing, and he's left in dirty clothes. He'll request a change of clothes too, if he doesn't automatically get some. He was the only one of us in the desert trying to stay clean in Afghanistan. Captivity won't change that obsession. That's when he'll get the note. I'm sure he's looking to and anticipating my next move."

Swallowing, Saundra nodded. "All my life, I've believed that if I had lived during that time, I would have never been a slave. I naively boasted that it wouldn't have happened today. We would never succumb as our ancestors did. I'm not nervous, but I am scared. You just said that this could get Saul killed. I know enough to know that everyone who had any knowledge of this abomination would be next. I—"

"—Daughter, you will prevail because you must. I don't fear for you, but I fear for what you will become if you fail to help. While you do, I will pray."

Opening his mouth to tell them it would be better to believe in themselves than a God who let the things he had seen in the service happen, Zachary, instead, held his peace. A wise person once told him just because it came into his mind didn't mean it had to go outside his mouth.

"Uh, yes, ma'am, you pray. Saundra, I won't meet with Saul, but can you get this word to him? If this works, he'll need to be ready for what's next. Tell him thank you."

Zachary handed her a specially coded message for Saul to place inside Bebop's clothing.

"Bebop knows this paper will dissolve in water." He then handed her a small blank sheet just like it. "He can send back his message to me on this one. When he does, don't call me. Simply place the message inside my trash can, under the garbage bag. Got it?"

Taking both sheets of paper, she placed them in her bra. Rosa spryly jumped up. "Oh no, Saundra. You already sweating. You put that message against them girls, and you gon' have a puddle of nothing."

"Ma!" Saundra scolded as she accepted the sandwich Ziplock bag her mother held in her direction. Saundra placed the messages inside the bag. She then arched her eyebrow and returned the message to her bra, patting it safe.

Watching the interaction between mother and daughter, Zachary chuckled.

Rosa looked over at him and smiled, "Operation Salvation begins."

Forehead scrunched, Zachary stood, making his way to the door. Of course, he didn't intend to call it any such thing, and he just hoped the name didn't catch on.

Chapter Nineteen

"It can't be; it can't be!" Sari yelled in her sleep, tossing in her straw bed, waking everyone in the room.

John squatted next to her, shaking her shoulder. "Sari girl, wake up."

Junie sat up, watching Sari open her eyes and look everywhere but at the two of them.

Uh-oh. Junie had a feeling this wasn't a dream she wanted to share with their papa.

"Fear ridin' your mind, girl. It gon' be a'ight. We gon' find a way out."

Trying to distract his father, Junie pleaded, "Papa, you promised to practice your words. You not pronouncing your endings, especially those with the letter *g*."

Looking perplexed at Junie, then with ire, he said slowly, "I am so sorry, Junie. Let's see if I can do better since I've been practicing for all of two days. I can promise you a whipping if you don't stop acting foolish. How's *dat*?"

Junie gulped. "That's . . . That's fine, Papa."

Behind his father's back, Sari put her hands together and mouthed thank you to her brother.

"I'm all right, Papa. Just a little nightmare. It's hard to let my mind relax here."

Nodding, John went back to his pallet. He adjusted his threadbare blanket over him and said into the dark, "Night, children."

Releasing his pent-up breath, Junie snuggled back under his covers. "Night, all."

Sari looked over at her brother, hunched her shoulders, and stared into nothing. Junie could see that she intended to stay up a little longer. He knew her distress was all tied to the mystery man. He also knew what Sari feared most: if her dreams come true, she would have to leave her Papa and him. In their short lives, they had learned love was rarely kind.

The dark room had no sunlight and little air.

The family timed morning by the banging of the door opening and the screaming of the stout, ruddy-faced man with no name.

It was the same each morning. "Move it, or lose it, baboons. Get your funky butts out—now!"

Then he pushed and prodded them along the way. If they were blessed, he didn't kick them. They had learned to wash what they could of their bodies at night because the morning was always rushed. This slavery that the lab had them in made no sense to them. They never had contact with any other enslaved people outside of their overseer. They could see people far off, backs bent, working in fields. But they could never get close to them. Bebop thought it was a hologram because he had never encountered them either. They were confused until he explained that they played moving pictures that appeared to be real people but weren't. Junie couldn't fathom this world. But he listened and studied what he could. He knew the delay was not punishment but time for preparation.

He remembered Ms. Mamie seeing the same strange items that he dreamed of. Now, he was here and had to allow his mind to stretch to the probability that God was doing something brand new.

But to what end?

All three tilled the dirt when another man, dressed like a planter, marched out to the field with determination and a sinister grin on his face. When they all stopped and looked at him, he stared hard at John and stopped short of coming closer.

"You, gal! Come with me," he shouted.

Sari gasped but quickly kept hitting her hoe at the dirt. Her long, wavy twists of hair bopped as she threw her body into her task.

Bebop stepped between them and, playing his role, asked, "What you'se need, suh? Mayhap I can hep?"

"Negra, get out of the way. This don't concern you. You one step away from working these fields yourself—or lying under them." Bebop's neck tensed, and his fingers tightened on the bullwhip. "Don't do it, boy. A whip ain't no fight against a bullet. Now, come on, gal, git!"

Sari reluctantly laid down her hoe and stepped around the wheelbarrel blocking her way. Dirt flew around her as John hit the packed ground with a hardened blow.

Sari grunted as the man grabbed her arm and half-dragged her across the grounds. When he got to the large cabin, he opened the door and threw her in, then slammed the door behind them.

No words were spoken about what just happened as a pool of tears filled Junie's eyes.

"I apologize that in the time you've been on this earth, men have not evolved to a better species of people. As a result, people have died for less."

Junie wiped his now bulging eyes. "You've killed before, Mr. Bebop?"

"Just Bebop, son."

"No, suh. He respect his elders. It be Mr. Bebop, Junie."

"Mr. Bebop, sir. In the war? Or does people just kill folk now, without a how-you-do?"

"Yes, it was in the war, and unfortunately, folk kills folk without a how-you-do too."

His eyes fixed at the cabin, John spoke in a deliberate, measured tone. "I've never had the freedom to give in to my rage, and I just had to let the fire in my belly eat me from the inside out." He then turned to Bebop. "A *man* gets tired."

Bebop's face registered the shared pain of impotence. Junie watched both and turned from the uncomfortable sight of their naked vulnerability.

"Papa, Mr. Bebop keep saying in this time, we not slaves. But we are."

"Yes, we are." Linking eyes with Bebop, John said, "You've never been caught and bound. But iffin' . . . sorry, the word is if. *If* a man can't go his own way, live like he wants to and he gets told what he can't say no to? He be a . . . my pardon." Exasperated, John wiped his sleeve across his brow. "He *is* a slave."

He then grabbed Junie by the shoulder and squeezed. "But this is for a short while, Junie. We'll escape again. And when we do, we'll not ever be slaves again. I promise."

"I don't have news yet. But my friend has never let me down. So I know we'll hear something any day now," Bebop promised.

John's legs spread wide, and his biceps flexed as he focused on the cabin. "It can't be too soon."

Junie followed his father's glower to the cabin, where the light flickered in the window. *Just hope it ain't too late.*

John shook in impotent rage. All the time they were on the Benson Plantation, Sari's skin had never shown one mark. Now, there were large finger bruises around her wrist and a dark rising lump on her cheek. Even her shift was torn. Sari sobbed in Junie's arms as he looked over her shoulder to his father for some help. He could see so many expressions across the older man's face that he could only pray that the good Lord Almighty came and rescued them soon.

Her sobs calming into sniffles, Sari whined, "It was so awful, Papa. That . . . that . . . he touched me and then I . . ." Sari straightened her body and lifted her head. "I fought, Papa! Fought like I be free. Kicked and scratched, even bit the hand that tried to hold me still."

John ran to her and hugged her hard. "You did good. Don't you feel bad, Sari. You did good, girl!" He hesitated, then asked in a low voice. "You spoilt?"

Shyly, peeking over at Junie, Sari briskly shook her head. "Some fool noise kept ringing. It be a sign from God, Himself. Because that smell-good man pushed me away and told that other man to bring me here and lock me in. So, I just lay here and wait for y'all day to be done. I had got myself quiet, but when you come through the door, my brave done left right out, and I started shaking like a leaf in a high wind. He don't smell so good now, Papa. His scent make me sick."

Patting her hand, John hugged her one more time. Junie came over and leaned against her, needing to touch her and know she was here as John moved away.

Junie watched his father turn his back on them and his shoulders hunch. They had seen so much, and this was the very thing that had made his father decide to run even before the voice spoke.

"Papa?" Junie called out.

John didn't turn but answered in a smothered voice, "Yeah, Junie?"

Junie then pulled his sister over to his father, and both put their arms around his back. Then softly, Junie said, "She fought back, Papa. Didn't lay down and let it happen. Mayhap we were in slavery. But the slavery no longer in us."

John turned and looked at them, a rising grin framed his chiseled jaw. "I was only seeing the bitter taste of what freedom cost, Junie. But every down has an up. We gon' think on these things."

Junie had heard that phrase somewhere else. He just couldn't pinpoint where. But he would do as his papa said: "Think on these things."

Chapter Twenty

Rushing down the corridor to Mr. Burstein's office, Zachary knew that Legend was back, and the men that decorated the hallway on their previous visit had doubled. Knocking and then entering immediately, Zachary approached the man who texted him an SOS text.

"How can I be of assistance, sir?"

Edgar's speech was strained, and he was sweating like it was a hundred degrees in the air-conditioned office. "Legend has informed us that they found an additional source which assures the senator that we are holding some prize here that belongs to him."

Legend rose from his chair where he was leisurely slouching and said, "No prize. We received word through one of my channels that three people of color were brought here dead and then were brought back to life from pre-Civil War times. It sounds like fantasy at best. But I was assured it was true. I told the senator that couldn't be because the Zachary Trumble I knew would never be involved in some low-down experiment where people were treated as lab rats. Am I right?"

Zachary knew two things. Legend always slouched before he pounced and that he had enough information to find the people, and then it would be the senator's ball game.

"Mr. Burstein has never shared any such thing with me. You searched this place yourself."

"Yes, we did. But before, I walked through as a friend. But that same birdy told me that some construction has been happening here. We are looking for the architect or the crew that worked on it."

Zachary blinked but smiled. "Then you'll have all your answers."

"It appears that they are all conveniently 'missing,' just like the lab technician whose family is currently rounding up a crew to find their kin or walk away with someone's blood on their hands. But since I know it won't be you, I pity the fool who will be their target," Legend said as he looked directly at Edgar Burstein.

Burstein wobbled as he sat. "Please assure the senator that there has been some mistake. As a matter of fact, I'll call him myself."

"Oh, he will not be accepting any more communications from you, and he will also not be renewing any more grants for your research center. He wanted me to relay the message that it is dangerous to bite the hand that feeds you. Starvation usually comes next."

Legend strolled to the door. "My men and I will take one more look around before we leave if you don't mind—or even if you do." He chuckled, then added, "Funny, since I was in the area, I stopped to see my man, Bebop. His house was deserted. Doesn't he work here anymore?"

Zachary frowned. "I meant to follow up with him after Human Resources said he called off. Not like him at all. But I figured it might be his wife or son or something. If his house is empty, maybe they all went out of town in an emergency. I'll try calling him. It'd be good for us all to get together again."

Legend opened the door, then hesitated. "Well well well. Frick doesn't know the whereabouts of Frack?" He then stepped through the door. "It would be good to get together, minus the bloodshed. Let's hope that happens."

The door slammed, and Zachary ogled Edgar. "You want to explain what's going on in my building? I can't keep people safe when I don't know the deal."

"Contrary to your thoughts, this is *my* building. Everything is fine. Your job is to protect and serve. Do what you were paid to do. And I was unaware that you were friendly with the one he calls Bebop."

"I'm friendly with all my men."

Edgar's bathroom door swung open to the right of his desk. Marilyn stepped into the middle of the room, and without greeting Zachary, she said, "I'll have the room, please—Now."

Zachary had leaned forward when she swung the door open and used her distraction to place a small device under the rim of the desktop.

Nodding, he pivoted and left the room. He hightailed it down to his office to listen. He had no idea how often Edgar had his office swept. However, he hoped the device would be pinned on Legend and not him when it was swept again and found.

Locking his door and putting in his earphones, Zachary pulled his transmitter booster out of the secret compartment in his desk.

There was static, and then, *"That mindless thing between your legs will cost you everything."*

"Marilyn, stop acting like a petulant child. What I do with my discovery is none of your business. Owners sample the wares all the time and often. I'm simply researching the emotions and mental state of the Black race. It's fascinating to watch how docile they are in captivity."

"I'm not sure how docile they are when I look at the scratches and bite marks on your arms before you covered them with your jacket, and I darted into the bathroom. And they ran before, so don't count them out. You're playing a dangerous game. Ditch them, take the cells and organs you need, and be done with them. Didn't you tell me someone wanted to pay top dollar for their hearts? You even have matches for their kidneys. Let's make this money."

"You know why we aren't together anymore?"

"Because you needed coke to keep it up?" she goaded.

"No. Because you were brute strength without knowing how to play the long game. Your time in M15 gave you skills, but you never understood strategy."

"Enlighten me to your strategy because that pretty little psychopath will skin you alive. And I mean that literally. I pulled his military records through some contacts, and he's bat crazy."

"No problem. I have my little toy soldier he can play with."

"No, Zachary is too decent to come against that one. Mark my words; you moving these people around on your make-believe checkerboard will be your ruin."

"I don't play games, Marilyn. I win at life. And my next overseas phone call with China will bring me millions. In four days, this will almost be over."

"What's the point of spending all this money on a fake plantation for two weeks of data?"

"First, it wasn't my money. I'm not stupid. Second, some people want *this data—groups with intentions beyond you and me. I am slowly turning up the heat on our guests, and today's tussle with the girl was just part of it."*

"What about William, the one they call Bebop?"

"That was the unexpected bonus in all of this. Having the data to watch a Black man help hold captive other Black people to save his own life? An ex-military Special Forces medal holder, no less. This information is priceless for the group who wants this data."

There was static, and then a door opened and closed, stopping all chatter.

Zachary lowered his head. The adrenaline pumping through his veins had him standing and moving around the room. It couldn't be called pacing because it was too erratic to have any specific pattern. He knew paranoid Edgar would probably find the bug before the day was out. But he now knew that everything had to be a go. They had to pull it all off the next day, or their window of opportunity would be gone. It was boots on the ground—beat feet.

They were all wrong about me. So, yes, I like to do the right thing, but I understood that the balance to that was sometimes very bad.

Chapter Twenty-One

The next morning, without the sun's warmth, the Bensons crossed the field, being barked at and prodded with a steel pic by their captor.

When they got close enough to their workstation, he cursed them and veered away. Then Sari said, "Look like Mr. Bebop waiting on us. I sure hope he have news."

The three of them hurried over to where Bebop stood near a barn door. "Today, you will muck out the stables, put fresh hay in, and then continue to till that plot of land for planting. John, since they now know of your iron works abilities, you will work on replacing the barn door."

John turned and examined the door hinges. "Nothing wrong with this door."

Bebop sighed, talking with his mouth almost closed. "No, nothing wrong, but we both know you'll do it anyway. Edgar Burstein is getting his kicks. There isn't anything you're doing that is useful. But don't get complacent. I'm seeing a lot of back-and-forth into his cabin down here, and believe you me, something big is going to happen, and when it does, no one will be left unscathed. This is the calm before the storm."

"Already done happened," John said.

Bebop peered at each one . . . until his gaze rested on Sari's face. "You all right?"

"I fought for me," she said with a winning smile. "I don't know about the next time, but this bruise is a medal, and I wear it proudly."

Bebop returned her smile and said, "You're speaking well."

Snorting, Sari chuckled, "Always could, just didn't. Most of my time was with Missus, and she talked my ear to the wall on most days. So I do all right."

Heart pounding, Junie picked up the pitchfork, and Sari pulled a fresh bale of hay over, and they got started. Bebop stood at attention, watching them when the man from earlier came into the barn.

"Boss said for you to push the trash and laundry over for pickup today. Big things coming, and he wants me in that meeting. Can't be helped. He said to remind you that he knows where your family lives."

Coming out of the barn, Bebop closed the door behind him.

John whispered, "Mind the cameras. Keep working."

All three continued to work, and when their stomachs rumbled, and that's all they could hear, the bell clanged for them to come out and eat. This was the part of the day that made them all scratch their heads. The food was excellent and nutritious, and they could have as much as they wanted. They ate well, twice a day. Bebop told them that it was so they stayed strong for whatever Mr. Burstein had planned. Junie felt like the pig being readied for a cookout. He knew it was coming, but he had to eat in the meantime.

He still couldn't hear from Heaven, and it made him anxious. The voice had never deserted him before. His father told him the voice hadn't abandoned him, that he was teaching Junie to build his faith. So Junie had to tell himself daily that God had not left them.

Looking up from his plate, Junie saw Bebop coming up to them. He then took his place behind them and said softly, "Help has come. Soon, we'll have a plan out of here. Don't eat too much. Don't want you too sluggish to move when it's time," he warned.

Returning to his office, Zachary caught Saul lying in wait. He was sweeping around his desk when Zachary walked in.

"Are you crazy?" Zachary asked after reviewing the security roster and noting Saul's picture, so he knew it was Saul in his office.

"Don't worry. Someone called off, and Saundra sent me up here as a substitute. If anyone checks, it'll check out."

"I don't care. Tell me why you risked this?"

Saul kept working and said, "I didn't need to leave a note because your friend, Bebop, was the one who met me at the elevator. I was running late, and he was running late, and it worked out."

"Why were you running late?"

Looking sheepish, Saul said, "Because I was scared to death."

"Wrong choice of words. Did Bebop read my message?"

"Yeah, he said to tell you, you can't sleep. Something's going down soon. He also said you can get them out the same way you got the message in."

Grinning, Zachary rubbed his hands together. "Whatever is going around that your coworker called in sick for just became an epidemic."

"You want to share what that means?"

"No, I don't. Just tell Bebop to have everyone ready the night of your next run. Let's go over your routine one more time so that I'm sure. You make a trip in the morning and drop off fresh clothing and then pick up the trash and soiled clothing that needs to be laundered, correct?"

"Yeah. I do it two days a week. Of course, there are a lot more people down there than before, so the loads are larger, and the cart is bigger. But it's still two days a week. Mr. Burstein is real fastidious, and those around him better be clean."

"When is your next run?"

"Two days from now, Friday."

"Plan to be ready tomorrow morning. We can't wait on Friday. Tell Bebop to be ready for tomorrow night. Tell him, Bangkok Blues. And, Saul, leave the fresh clothes, but instead of bringing both carts up the elevator, dump the soiled clothes over the garbage and only bring up the trash cart. Then leave the laundry cart covered in green burlap by the bushes. I'll leave the burlap in your car. When you get up here, transfer the clothes to another laundry cart and take it to the pickup location. Oh, and, Saul, bring your own lunch to work for the next couple of days."

Puzzled but indicating he heard him, Saul picked up his push broom and cleaners cart and rushed out of the room.

Later that day, before the dinner service, Zachary made his way through the industrial kitchen, speaking to the staff and making it obvious he was checking entryways. On the way out, he bumped into the head chef as he stirred a large stock pot of delicious soup.

"Sorry, big guy. That soup smells amazing." Zachary leaned over the pot, waving his hand back and forth to smell the aroma. He completely blocked the chef from seeing what he was doing. Then feeling a push from behind, Zachary stepped back from the pot, "Hey, I'm going. You can't blame a guy for trying at least to smell something that's going to be this delicious."

"Not my problem. Strict orders that these meals are strictly for medical staff and our special guests," the chef remarked, throwing more seasoning in the pot.

"Guests?" Looking down at his clipboard, Zachary pretended to read it. "I don't see any guests written here."

"Again, not my problem. You don't come in here often, and now that you're here, you're a nuisance. I'd like you to leave. We have a dinner menu to finish. I have salmon to prepare." Chef snipped as he shooed Zachary out of his kitchen.

Raising his hands from his pockets, Zachary waved goodbye. "I can see where I'm not wanted; I'm out."

A purposeful stride moved him down the long hallway. Zachary slid to the camera's blindside, took the small vial out of his pocket, and threw it away. Saundra would arrange for the garbage on this floor to be dumped before anyone could check any trash bins. Tomorrow, Edgar would be suspicious but too busy to prove or act on his lack of proof.

Mission accomplished. Now, let's pray . . . No, let's hope that Saul gets word to Bebop, and Bebop remembers Bangkok Blues.

Chapter Twenty-Two

Hearing a crunching noise, Junie jumped when a figure in the dark crept into their cabin. Not being able to sleep after the attack on his sister, he had been staring into nothingness and talking to God, who remained silent for the first time in his life. He felt like an amputee whose missing limb only now made him realize how precious it was for his quality of life.

Junie prepared to pounce and then yell to give his father time to jump into a fight they would win.

Instead, the figure whispered, "Shush, it's me, Junie. Bebop."

"Mr. Bebop?" Junie whispered. "What are you doing here?"

"Kindly move as quickly as you can and cover your sister's mouth," he whispered back.

"What?"

"Junie, move!"

Junie scrambled over to Sari and covered her mouth. She woke up swinging. "Hush, Sari girl, it's me. Sometin's happenin'. Bebop is here."

Sari sat up and pushed Junie away. "Must be. You lost your precious 'g's when you spoke. I'm good."

John then spoke into the dark. "Bebop, you can loose me now. I'm awake."

Using his flashlight, Bebop illuminated the darkness. "Good. Listen, there's a reason I dropped your soup before you could eat it tonight.

Every guard, medical personnel, and regular staff has stomach poisoning. Either they're in the infirmary, or they're finally sleeping. We're leaving here now."

"Now?" John said. He looked around, grabbed each of his children, and hurried to the door. "We ready."

Bebop went in front of them, and seeing the way clear, he ran, and they followed as he made it to the elevator. Then pulling a large clothes cart covered in green burlap from between two tall bushes, he motioned for them to climb in.

John went in first, then Sari, and then Junie.

Muffled from under him, Sari moaned, "Junie, you stink."

Smirking, Junie said, "We all stink."

"It's going to be even worse. Just give me a minute." Bebop covered Junie with the burlap and added soiled clothes from earlier, which Saul had left behind for that purpose.

"I'm going to be sick, Papa. It smells Gawd awful," Sari sobbed as she moved restlessly under Junie.

Junie could hear her gasping for air as she only took on more foulness. "It's worse than anything . . ." Junie groaned.

"Be quiet!" Bebop hissed. "Your whining is going to get all of us caught, and I want out of here alive as much as any of you."

They got off the elevator on the right floor, and Saundra was waiting for them. She handed Bebop a change of clothes and took over, pushing the cart. Quickly changing into the cleaning services jumpsuit, Bebop put on the baseball cap and stayed out of direct sight of the cart. Going around the corner to the back exit doors, a van with the cleaning services logo was on hand. Wheeling the cart up the ramp and into the truck, Bebop quickly helped Junie and the rest of the Bensons out of the cart. He handed them their change of clothes from the floor and advised them to change into the jeans and T-shirts quickly. Next, he gave them packages of cloth wipes and pulled one out to show them how they worked.

"It's the best we can do. And wiping your bodies down is important. You don't want people to remember you because you smelled bad."

He then handed them scissors to cut their locks of hair. "It's easy to describe who they knew; harder to find you if you don't match their descriptions."

Climbing out of the van's cabin, Bebop watched Saundra run back to the exit doors as she waved as she usually would and mouthed, "Good luck." Then shutting the van door, Bebop ran to the passenger's side and hopped in.

Turning to thank his rescuer, Bebop grinned wide when Zachary turned and winked as he pulled off. "You devil!" Bebop crowed.

"That I am," Zachary said. Then quieting, he asked, "You good?"

"As good as I can be when in the clutches of a certified madman. He's really sick. Getting the family out just in time was necessary, man." Bebop held up a phone. I stole this from one of his head people. "Man, these guys have so much mayhem planned, I don't know where to start. But it's all on this," he said, shaking the phone.

"Won't he be looking for it?" Zachary asked as he slowly drove the van up the drive toward the fence that would lead them out of the Burstein Labs compound. He was making sure he was slow and steady, not drawing any attention.

"He was occupied over the toilet when I stole it. By the time he realizes I'm missing *and* his phone, he'll put two and two together. But he still won't report it. Edgar was so paranoid that he forbid any electronics in the Boiler Room. That was their code name for the most ratchet, diabolical plan since eugenics."

"I'm just glad you remembered Bangkok Blues."

"How could I forget? We didn't have to use one bullet after spiking those terrorists' soup. They almost walked out with their hands raised in surrender."

"Those hands were busy. They were moving from covering their mouths to their butts."

Laughing, Bebop sobered. "My family . . . You get them out?"

"First thing I did. Including your dear Mother Sweat, who never ceases to amaze me, even though she shoves y'all's God down my throat."

"He's your God too, stubborn fool," Bebop sighed. "Who you think made sure your plan went off without a hitch?"

Approaching the gate, both Zachary and Bebop jumped when the lab's piercing alarm system sounded. Looking into the rearview mirror, Zachary looked for the approaching vehicle that would be rushing to cut them off. Instead, he saw multiple figures in military formation, storming the building, Legend at the lead. Pushing on the gas and hightailing it out of there, Zachary floored it.

"We got to make as much progress as we can before Legend realizes the cleaning truck leaving the compound was leaving with his contraband."

Reaching under the seat, Bebop pulled out an AK-47. He rubbed it like an old friend and nodded to Zachary. "Let's make this work."

Their occupants in the back were worried about the gravel shooting from under the tires.

"Papa, how we moving so fast?" Sari cried out.

"Don't know, Sari, but it's like we flying."

Junie thought hard. "Papa, I dreamt of seeing these different-shaped steel boxes moving fast. Mamie saw them too." Junie paused, then said, "I think we inside of one, Papa."

Grinning, he yelled, "Oooh-wee! We is almost flying. And we *free*."

All three smiled . . . and then frowned as the van slowed down to a crawl, and they could feel them turning off the road. Then they stopped.

They heard the sound of feet running. Then the van door opened, and Bebop hurried them out of the van. "Don't have a lot of time. Another group is after you, and we don't know if they're the only ones." Then pointing to a large horse trailer with a horse in the back, he told them to get in the trailer.

The driver's door opened in the cleaning van, and Zachary got out with a walkie-talkie in his hand that rang gunshots and yelling from its speakers. "We don't have much time." Walking over to them, he rapidly gave as much information as possible. "Name's Zachary. This is not the meeting place I meant for you. I've passed this man on this road a thousand times as he picks up his cargo. My car's tire got a screw in it here. I noted it took the man about twenty minutes to complete his paperwork. This is not perfect, but this is the best we can do. While the man is inside, you climb into the back of the trailer. I'll find out where it's headed later." He then handed them a burner phone. "It's on. I left instructions on how to use it on the page I have open in case something happened, and we had to separate. Can anyone read?"

"I can read, sir," Junie said.

Remaining quiet, Sari half-hidden behind her father, they all began to move. John went up first and made sure he quieted the horse. He then pulled Junie up, keeping Sari's face turned from Zachary. Sari was the last to get into the trailer. Finally, looking up, she and Zachary froze.

"You!" they said in unison.

The trailer's driver, a lanky cowboy hat-wearing man, spat tobacco from his lips and then was met with a loud Bebop. "Man, I couldn't help but stop and see that beauty of a horse I could spot from the road. I'm Mississippi, born and bred, and you don't see horse flesh like that these days. Sho' make me miss home. My pappy worked for Mr. Embers, and he bred them well. I used to lock up the trailers whenever they took them on the road. Sure would be an honor if you'd let me do it one more time. Sho' do miss my pappy."

Scratching his head under his cowboy hat, the stranger said, "We good ol' boys got to stick together. I'll just go over with you while you do the honors."

Zachary and Sari's concentration was broken hearing them come closer. Then speaking with tenderness, Zachary said, "I'll find you." He lifted her and stepped aside as Bebop closed the gate.

Standing between Bebop and the cowboy, Zachary said, "City fellow myself. I don't get it. But he yelled fool crazy to stop, so I did. We better get to moving, man."

The cowboy leaned over and yanked the lock. Then satisfied, he tipped his hat and moved to his driver's door.

Bebop yelled over. "Name is George. Safe travels. How far you got to go?"

"Colonial Williamsburg. Y'all be good now," he said as he swung into the cab, and they went to the van.

After closing their doors and returning to the road, the van was silent. Then finally, Bebop said to a dazed Zachary, "What was that all about back there? Sari's a beautiful but fragile girl, and you're a married man. *Not* a good combination."

Breathing in and out as slowly as he could, Zachary was working not to hyperventilate. "Sari," he breathed. "I've been in love with that woman since I was thirteen. That's my wife." Then biting his lip, he mugged at Bebop. "And I just might start believing in your God."

"Man, you not making sense. Not that I won't thank anything or anyone that brings you closer to acknowledging Him. But why now?"

"Because only a supreme God could bring the love of my life across time."

Chapter Twenty-Three

The trailer ate up the miles as the Bensons looked out between the slates in the back and marveled at the freeway.

Excited, Junie said with awe, "This is what I saw; this is my dream. Papa, it's all true. We in another time."

"Don't seem real to me. But nothing since I woke up seems real. Papa, I got something to tell you too," Sari said, her voice trembling.

John rubbed the horse more to anchor himself than to calm the animal. His face broadcast the bewilderment of too much happening too quickly. "Right now be a good time to put my mind on something else. Go head, chile."

Twisting her hands, she opened her mouth and closed it before finally pushing out her words. " I know you always believed me to be addled-brained. But when I was just a little bit, Mama told me never to let on I had good sense. She said there was power in keeping my own counsel. She told me her looks drew the wrong person to her, but it was her smarts that fascinated him."

In the silence that followed, Junie could see the expressions flit across his father's face. First puzzlement, then a dawning of understanding, then hurt and sadness.

Turning to look at her more directly, John said, "Junie hinted at some of this. Getting power any way we can when we are powerless is wise.

And your mama was a woman of wisdom. But why hide your nature from me? From Junie?"

"Because if I could hide myself from you, I could learn to be someone else enough that it would become second nature to me. Mama said the burden of a colored woman is to be strong for her menfolk. I knew they were planning to match me with someone. But I was working on Missus so that it would be on my own terms. I couldn't press that on you, Papa."

Junie gave an exasperated sigh. "That's just plain dumb, Sari. How you think you gon' control what can't be controlled?"

"Junie's right, Sari. Missus would do what Jacob told her to. There were times she was just as much under his thumb as the rest of us. Only his sons might have made a plea on your behalf."

Shyly, she looked down. "I was working on them too."

Leaning, then falling forward even further when the trailer changed lanes, John said, "You speaking too low, gal. I know you didn't say what I thought you said. There's no way you were sweet-talking them Benson boys."

Huffing and crossing her arms, Sari pouted. "Papa, we in a whole other time. Them boys dead and gone."

"But your new beau not," Junie said. "Papa didn't see, but I did. Why'd you lose your thoughts when you saw the other man that rescued us?"

Looking back and forth between Sari and Junior, John growled. "More secrets? What man?"

Junie didn't want his father to be further hurt by secrets kept. "Sari been dreaming about some man for years, Papa. Dreams got more real since she woke up."

"Sari?" John said with a timber in his voice that he *never* used with his children.

Wincing, Sari clasped her hands together. "I can't help my dreams, Papa. Started when I was young, and I didn't understand them then. Never saw his whole face at first, just his eyes, always watching me. They were kind eyes. I thought maybe he would come to the plantation, and I would look at every new arrival, slave and free. But he not there. Then ..."

"Then?" John prompted her to get on with it as his jaw became more rigid the longer she spoke.

"Right before we got to Miz Mamie's, the night after I claimed Junie's pants, I saw him full. Papa, I think I even dreamed of him while we slept through the years!" In wonder, she continued, "Don't seem possible. We woke up here, and then dreams became more. And, and . . . How could I tell you he's a white man, Papa? The white man that came to help us."

Sitting down with a thump, John wiped his brow. The movement of the trailer and the neighing of the horse had him rubbing the mare in a circular motion.

John focused on Junie and then Sari. "Never had much control over anything. Most I've done as a father is helped you run when running was all we could do, and Junie helped with that figuring. Couldn't have pride in much because much was never given to me. But I thought I knew my children. Thought if danger was near, I would at least be someone you could come to. Now, I've woken up to truths I didn't know I needed."

"No, Papa. No!" Sari cried. "Mama didn't trust I could pull it off unless I never dropped the playacting. She admonished me for years to keep my wit about me. She didn't never want y'all to treat me like they treat Junie. Because then owning pretty wouldn't be someone's only reward."

Junie thought on it. "I remembered they used to say about Sari, 'least she pretty.' Is that what you're saying?"

"Yes, Missus dress me up, prance me around. Then barked at me behind doors that I'm addled-minded. It kept her feeling that she was better than me, even though I was already a slave. They used to laugh about me right in front of my face. 'Oh, dumb Sari.' 'Flighty Sari.' But I waited, and I learned, Papa."

John stiffened, his face still like granite, his shoulders tense.

Sari stretched her hand out, and John took her smaller one in his. "I love you, Papa. Please don't be mad. Mama thought a girl-child had to have wits to keep *herself* secure, as much for those who loved her as for herself."

Junie lay back against the trailer wall, hoping to change the subject and give them all some relief from the tension. "I wonder how long it's going to take to get where we're going."

"Open up that thing he gave you, Junie. He said it held a note inside for you. Read it, so we can know what's coming."

Junie opened his phone and touched the button on the side like he was instructed to do. The cell's screen lit up, and Junie touched the icon as he was told. He then read quietly and then read it again to be sure.

"This says that he was taking us to a place where we would meet up with some people he trusts. It says in case we get lost from each other that I should take off the back cover of this phone and use what's inside to hide until he calls this number and comes for us."

Peeling the phone case away from the phone, Junie pulled out five crisp hundred-dollar bills. Fingering them, he then said, "According to the rest of this note, we should find a real cheap motel, *not* a hotel. He says we should stay out of sight until he can come for us."

"Bebop told us about motels during our schooling from him. They outside, not inside rooms, and usually cheaper. Let's get some sleep. Whatever we decide to do, we need to have our wits about us," John said as he lay against the opposite wall from Junie.

Junie woke first when he felt they were no longer moving. The trailer was pulling onto a dirt road that ran along the side of what looked like a corral. Then waking everyone with his finger on his mouth to stay quiet, he peered out into the darkening day.

"Running late there, ain't ya?"

They could hear someone call out to the man they called Cowboy.

Next, they could hear the opening and closing of the truck's door and feet clumping against gravel.

"Darndest thing how my day got away from me. But I can unload her for you and settle up with you in the morning if that'll help any."

"Sure would. My wife already called me twice. It's my daughter's birthday, and they're waiting on me to sing the song and light the candles."

"Hey, man, I get it."

John pulled them all to the very back of the trailer in front of the horse. She neighed, and John softly rubbed her on her forehead. He whispered into her ear. Then he heard the lock disengaged, and the other man called out to him before Cowboy could pull open the gate.

"Hey, if you could just sign this, we can do the rest tomorrow. But boss all about the signatures being done at the time of delivery."

Cowboy could be heard saying, "Sure 'nough," as he walked away.

Immediately, John, Sari, and Junie scooted, then jumped out of the trailer and climbed over the corral fence, lying on the ground.

"Hey, did you hear that?" Cowboy said, walking to the back of the trailer and looking around.

"Nah, the only thing I can hear is the echo of my lady yelling at me because I'm late. Can you take her to the barn so that I can close up? Thanks."

Cowboy stood looking at the wide-open gate, then at the mare. "Come on, girl," he said as he coaxed her out of the trailer. He then mumbled, "Losing my ever-picking mind. I'm gon' sleep till afternoon. I need it."

When Cowboy pulled the horse away, John whispered, "Just stay here. Man said he was leaving. We wait on him to go."

After the trailer pulled off, all three stood and brushed themselves off. Looking around, they could see a barn and other buildings they didn't recognize.

"I don't know what these other buildings are, but I do know what a barn is, and it looks like a good place to get some sleep until tomorrow. You think you can use that thing to find what the man called a motel?"

"Sounds good, Papa," Sari said.

Junie climbed over the corral fence and waited for the others to follow. His father taking the lead, they went over to the barn and pulled open the door. It was clean and the most enormous barn they had ever seen. Settling in, Junie took out the cell phone and looked again at the note. He started hitting icons and seeing the most wonderful and some very worrisome things.

"Look, Papa," Junie said, showing his father a TikTok video with half-dressed people jerking and gyrating to hard, thumping rhythms.

"My word!" Sari exclaimed, hiding her face with her hands. "Where's the rest of her clothes?"

"Sari, you bet not ever," John groused, his eyes enlarged as he glued them to the small screen.

They saw colored folk calling themselves Black holding up signs and demanding out loud to be treated better. Junie was fascinated with those signs that stated, "Black Lives Matter."

Imagine that.

Fascinated, he accidentally ran his finger over the screen, and new images and videos played.

"Not so sure you should be looking at those," John stated with resolve.

Junie was loathed to stop now. He couldn't help himself. The tiny screen called him like a siren to a man at sea. "But, Papa, how will we know what's out there if we don't learn?"

Junie gave Sari a pleading look, and she felt compelled to support his case. "If it will help any, I've seen enough, Papa. And somebody has to know what world we living in now."

"I thought Bebop did a good job of telling us." Seeing Junie's hunger for the moving pictures was real, John sighed. "Just a little longer, Junie; no more," he said, turning on his side. He was soon snoring in exhaustion.

Close behind him, Sari mumbled and sighed in her sleep as she turned over.

Obedient, an hour later, eyes tired and blurry, Junie lay with his hands behind his head, looking up at the barn's rafters. He thought about their journey and wondered out loud. "I don't know what tomorrow will bring, or even if my voice will return. But even when I couldn't hear you, you got us this far. I have to believe you will take us the rest of the way."

John's voice answered in the night. "That's faith, son. And maybe that's why you couldn't hear Him. You had to learn to trust Him. Most folk can't hear a voice, Junie. You like the rest of us now. believing what you can't know for sure."

"I hope Junie voice come back. I like somebody knowing something! Humph, all the same to you, can we go back to sleep?" Sari griped.

John chuckled. "That I can do."

Closing his eyes, Junie prayed some more. At that moment, he understood just because he couldn't hear the voice didn't mean the voice couldn't hear him.

Chapter Twenty-Four

When Junie opened his eyes, his father was already standing at the barn door, peeking out of its slight opening. Sari was pulling straw out of her hair and smiled when she saw he was awake.

"Land sakes, Junie. We gon' have to take that phone from you. How long did you watch it before you fell asleep?"

"Sari girl, this world is miraculous and sinful all at the same time. That thing had Betunde voodoo all over it. Had me stuck to it, even when sleep called me."

Running over on feet light for a man of his size, John said, "Let's go. No one's out yet. But if the horses is up, they'll be here soon to muck out their stalls. I'll go first and send out a bird call if I see anyone. Stay alert now."

John ran to the door, looked right and left, and then he slipped out. Sari followed, running to her right near the bushes and the dirt road leading out. Behind her, Junie brought up the rear. Unfortunately, his shoes were not a perfect fit, and he stumbled when they pinched his toes.

"Hey there, kid. Hey!" he heard behind him.

Junie took off, sore toe and all. The voice behind him cursed, but the man did not follow him. It was lucky for them that he did not see Sari or John. Junie was hoping they just thought it was some kid and not worth the chase.

After walking through a small warehouse area, they came to what looked like small shops. And although they were in jeans and T-shirts, they saw people opening their shops in clothes better suited for the era they came from.

"Papa, why do all these places look like home?" Sari asked as she twirled around in a circle.

"I'm not sure what I'm seeing," John murmured.

Junie took out his phone and typed in the name of the shop in front of him. His late-night exploring had given him more knowledge of how the device worked.

Reading what came up, he said, "Colonial Williamsburg is a vacation place where people come to enjoy times past. And it says here that they dress in period pieces and act out skills and a past way of life."

"Uh-uh. I can't believe we ended up in a place where people gon' be pretending to be slaves," Sari said.

"Plain foolishness. But we know how to be what they *pretending* to be. Maybe we should stay here awhile. Blend in just fine," John mused.

Junie put the phone in his jean pocket. "Wonder when he's going to call."

With an anxious-to-see-him-again face, Sari said, "Me too."

John then stopped on the sidewalk between two opening storefronts and pulled Sari aside. "I didn't speak on him being a white man because my first thought was to tell you never. But I bit my tongue because that was fear and slave talk." Exhaling, John continued, "If I believe that we free, then that include free to love who you want to love. I just want you to make sure, Sari, that the love is a sticking-through-thick-and-thin love. Because I got a feeling from everything I'm seeing, your kind of love still come against some strong hate, even in this new world."

"Some things still not so new, are they, Papa?" Sari said before putting her arm through her father's and then Junie's. "Good thing I don't have to face anything alone. Let's find some food. I'm hungry."

Grin wide, Junie made a wide stride as they moved up the sidewalk. All the while, in the back of his mind, he wondered where the man called Zachary was.

Chapter Twenty-Five

Zachary heard the birds chirping merrily away. His window was rolled down to feel the breeze in his hair. He tapped his fingers rhythmically on the steering wheel. He loved oldies music, and the fact that the song "Sara Smile" was playing made him dizzy with longing.

Sarah.

A little more time with Bebop before he dropped him off gave him more information about the Bensons. Namely, one gorgeous woman named Sarah, but her family had always called her Sari. She was twenty, well, not twenty. Actually, she was one hundred eighty-three years old. *Sheesh!*

After Zachary dropped Bebop at his meeting point, he was anxious to get to his dream come true. He had met *her*. In person. In technicolor so brilliant, it stole his breath and made his heart skip two beats. It hadn't beat right since. An EKG would validate it had lost its ability to synchronize with his body's needs. He needed *her*. The girl of his dreams in the middle of a drama-filled mess. But he couldn't be happier. All these years, he looked for his green-eyed dream girl. Then he met Sylvia. He thought she was his answered prayer—but was duped—when she became the nightmare to his unanswered hope. Now, he had truly found her, and he only had to keep her and hers alive and well, a duty he had already sworn he would do. He just hoped they had made it to Colonial

Williamsburg without mishap. Everything they had done was all by the seat of their pants, and any of it could go left before he reunited with Sarah.

Picking up his phone, he called his attorney. "Hey, man, glad I reached you. I need you to push my divorce through as hard and as fast as you can. I don't want to wait any longer than necessary to be free."

"You already had me pushing it through. You want more push?" his attorney asked.

Watching the road, Zachary said, "Yes—shove it. I need to be free—yesterday."

"You sound like a man ready to start a new chapter in your life."

Seeing his exit, Zachary said, "Think bestselling romance novel. Let's call it *Sarah*."

Giving a shrill whistle, his attorney said, "Don't do it, man. Keep things clean on your end."

"Advice denied. Just get her done." Hanging up the phone, he slowly approached his destination.

He needed to switch cars, and his boys had left his replacement ride with a few surprises in the trunk for him here.

Zachary was walking to the car when he realized he was not alone. He didn't know how Marilyn had found him, but he was halfway inside the vehicle, which had been stashed at the abandoned gas station parked among other abandoned cars scattered throughout the property, when she stepped out with three hulking goons backing her.

"How'd you find me?" Zachary shouted, not caring to play the game that they were not on to him.

Waving him away from his car door with her gun, she said, "I'm trained to find you. Where's our property?"

Hands held in the air, Zachary said, "Property? You sleeping for more than a century, aren't you? We aren't allowed to *own* people anymore, or did you miss basic government in your high school? Obviously, our school system sucks."

"Don't be dense. This world belongs more than ever to the power brokers who very rarely look like them. And don't confuse me with the rabid right-wingers out here touting nonsense. Everything to me is dollars, and that makes sense." Pointing her gun for him to move to her car, she continued, "Eugenics? The notion that we are inherently created biologically superior to be better than others? Nazi propaganda. That's just a way for greedy men to say to poor, insecure people that they were born to be the greater race. And while those people gathered to protest anything that might further those they believed were born beneath them, their own pocket of blessings was being fleeced. Their medical care, their wages, their housing . . . See, they're so busy being one-track-minded that they missed the train running right through their homes, the money train. Guess who's not on it?"

Rolling his neck to stay loose, Zachary snorted, "You guys are pitiful. Every war in the world was fought for power and money. Every cure for a disease has been buried because somebody would get richer off others *not* getting well. We breathe filth because the very nature God planted to cleanse our air, man ripped from the earth."

Clapping her hands while holding the gun in one hand, Marilyn said, "Oh, honey, I never took you for a bleeding heart believer."

Grumbling, Zachary said, "It's a recent thing. But with your arrival, maybe I moved too fast—"

Bang, bang, bang.

The man next to Marilyn fell to the ground, a red river running from the gaping wound in his chest. Marilyn dove for cover, and the two other guys swung and rapidly began to return fire.

Zachary made a zigzag sprint for the car door he had left open, dived in, and slammed the door shut. Then lying flat across the seat, he found the keys hidden under the driver's side. Hearing shots overhead, he jumped up, put the key in the ignition, and peeled off.

Chanting out loud, "Not now, Lord. Not. Now," Zachary looked in his rearview mirror and saw a black Charger peel off behind him. As his foot pushed down on the accelerator, he slowly smiled because this old hooptie had bite in her. "Thank you, Lord. Thank you, boys! Hooyah!" Whatever enhancements had been placed under his car's hood caused it to shoot out of there like an Indy 500 Racer. Hearing an explosion, he looked behind him and saw the black car on its side, smoke curling overhead as Marilyn stood there wide-legged with a launcher on her shoulder.

Thank you, God. Maybe I should just wait and see what else you pull off, Zachary thought as he screeched up the road. Using his rearview mirror to search behind him, he no longer saw a car trailing him. Knowing that Legend and Marilyn were now both pursuing him was not something he wanted to think about. Then Mother Sweat's last message to him floated through his mind. She said, *"The person who chases two rabbits catches none."* But what if she really meant, *"Two foxes who chase one rabbit end up hungry"*?

Zachary bellowed out loud, "Yes, make it so. Let them keep fighting each other."

He could only hope that the shootout lasted long enough for him to make his next move.

Ten minutes later, eleven miles away, Zachary pulled into a residential area. It was an old part of town, and the streets still had alleys. Rolling down an alley, Zachary noticed a garage with the door ajar and a five-year-old Malibu sitting inside. Pulling over, he snuck around the side of the house and didn't see any lights or signs of inhabitants inside.

Maybe someone works nights or, better yet, is out of town.

Sneaking back inside the garage, he hotwired the car, exchanged it for the vehicle Marilyn and her goons would be looking for, got his duffle out of the car's trunk, and shut the garage door. A plus-size hot-pink hoodie lay on the front seat, a blinged-out Fat Girls Rule, and a baseball cap sat on the dashboard as decoration. Pulling off the cleaning company's jumpsuit, he put on the baseball cap and the hoodie and threw the jumpsuit in a dumpster a mile away. He then pulled onto the freeway and headed to Colonial Williamsburg.

He knew Legend. His friend wouldn't rest until he found them. Saddened that he would finally have that showdown and find out who was the best, Zachary put his car on cruise and let the miles get eaten behind him. He only hoped his last moments were spent in rhinestones and hot pink.

Chapter Twenty-Six

"Junie, you can put the phone down for a minute and enjoy your food," John said.

"It's just all so interesting." Junie turned the screen and showed his father what he was reading. "We had a colored president, Papa. No, wait. They say Black or African American now."

"They call us Black just like that? That's not polite—is it, Papa?" Sari said.

"A president?" John beamed, then he slowly frowned. "Looks like what we fought against, they embraced. That music on some of the moving pictures—"

"—Video or reels, Papa," Junie said.

"They teaching you to interrupt your elders on there too, boy?"

"No, sir."

John nodded in satisfaction. "All right then . . . videos. The music calling women female dogs and calling us names we used to run from in our heads. I don't rightly understand the right of it."

Sari used her napkin to pat her lips. "Me neither. But this food taste good. These eggs and sausage is right delicious," she said as she popped a piece of biscuit slathered in butter and strawberry jam into her mouth.

"I think you can taste food better when you free," Junie said, watching the smacking going on at the table.

Junie laid the phone down and picked up his fork. Taking a bite, he grinned. He then looked around. Every race of customers sat in the large restaurant specializing in organic and grass-fed food. Before he could comment on it, he and his family all jumped when the phone on the table vibrated as it rang.

John picked up the phone and placed it in front of his face. Then speaking loudly, he yelled, "This is John."

Tapping the table, Junie pointed to a man at the next table, speaking with the phone on his ear in a low tone. "Got it," John said, lifting the cell to his ear.

He heard Zachary saying, "Hello, hello?"

"Hello. This is John," he said, clearing his throat several times.

"Are you all alright?"

"Yes, and just done with breaking our fast," John said.

"Great, you've eaten. I have a tracker on your phone. Meet me at Palace Green in front of the Playbooth Theater. Ask your waitress for directions. It will be within walking distance."

Getting the money from his pocket, John picked up the bill and waved their waitress over as he had seen others do.

Handing her the hundred-dollar bill, he asked, "Can you please bring our sandwiches? We're ready to go. And we're in a hurry. Can you tell us which way is Palace Green at the Playbooth Theater? Please, ma'am?"

He had decided wherever they ended up staying the night, they would not be coming back out. So, he had ordered sandwiches, and they came with something called chips. No strangers to being hungry, they felt it would be enough.

"Sure thing. It's really simple. When you leave here, go down three blocks, make a right and then one block up, make a left, and the theater is on the left-hand side of the street." Then looking at each shocked expression, she smiled. "How about I write it down? I'll be right back. I believe your order is up," she said as she picked up their plates and walked away.

Junie looked around and said softly, "Papa, she was so nice. She didn't act any kind of way with us being colored. I think people are leaving money on the table if they did a good job. The bill had a line on it for something called a tip."

Discussing it, all three looked stressed in not wanting to give too little or too much. But when the ten-dollar change came back from the bill with neatly written directions, John decidedly placed money on the table.

"We need to keep track of everything we use so that we can pay this man back," John said sternly to both children. "We not gon' start our new lives beholden to anyone." John then looked at Sari. "Even if he is sweet on my baby girl."

Blushing, Sari stood, and they all went outside and followed the directions Junie read. When they got close to the theater, John turned back and told them to wait in the alcove of a shop selling timepieces. He wanted to go ahead and make sure it was not a trap. Then with large strides, he purposely marched up the street.

"I'm going to go inside real quick and look at the timepieces, Sari."

Watching John's fading figure, Sari said, "Junie, Papa said wait right here."

"Aww, girl, I'll be right back. You can see me in the window."

Standing there looking after her father in the street now filled with tourists, Sari lost sight of him.

She was concentrating so hard she didn't see the tall, stocky man who slid up behind her and slurred in her ear, "You looking for me?"

Jumping back, Sari stammered, "N-No." Then holding her hand out to keep him from getting close, he jerked her forward.

"I think you were. How about you go with me for a little walk?"

Sari was appalled. She saw people moving by, yet this man was talking to her as though they were alone, not in the midst of a crowd. Then, before she could scream, a car door slammed, and she heard the sound of running feet.

Zachary snatched the man's arm, pulling him away from her. "What is wrong with you? You don't know her!" Holding his hand out, he caught hers and pulled Sari to his side. Sniffing the air, Zachary said, "You're drunk? It's noon. Get some—"

"—Ray? Is that you?" A blond woman said, holding the hand of a towheaded toddler. "What are you doing *now*, Ray? Did you hit on that girl? Ray? I promise I'll leave you if you don't get it together and stop drinking. Your brother's wedding was only yesterday, for goodness' sake. I'm ready to get on the road and leave here. Ray? Ray? You 'bout to be beat up by a man in pink, blinging *Fat Girls Rule*. You just soooo embarrassing." Then pulling the man by his polo shirt as he stumbled behind her, she stormed and screeched as she went up the street. "You wait until I tell Daddy. I'm just done . . ."

Standing there when they turned back, Junie and John had a baffled look on their faces. "What just happened?" Junie said.

"Everybody get in the shuttle, please," Zachary said. "We have miles to cover and two different enemies stalking us."

They all scrambled in, and as they went down the street one way, Zachary yelled, "Duck!"

John's reflexes were slower than a child's, so Zachary had to push him down in the seat. He then threw his hoodie back over his baseball hat. Keeping his face averted, Zachary saw Legend drive right by, looking up and down the street. Getting good at driving with his eyes peeled on his rearview mirror, he saw the car do a U-turn and head back up the street. . . searching.

"How is he driving in Colonial Williamsburg, where there are not supposed to be any cars at this time of day?" Zachary mumbled.

Senator!

Taking his shoes off, Zachary turned the corner and threw them out the window. He turned at the next corner and saw Legend moving fast up behind him.

His breathing erratic, he looked at the watch his grandfather left him that he always wore, taking it off. Then he threw it out the window. "Sorry, Pops," he groaned.

Making another turn and getting in front of another shuttle load of tourists, he said, "Stay down until I say otherwise."

Seeing he lost his trackers, Zachary headed out of town.

Making one more turn to lead them to the freeway, he ran right into Legend's car, idling by the freeway entrance.

Flooring it, Zachary took off with Legend and his car full of mercenaries in tow. Zachary knew they wouldn't shoot because they wanted his passengers alive. So he swerved, muttering at the slowness of the shuttle, and then looked for any opening to lose his tail.

Junie sat up. "Mister—"

"Get down—" Zachary yelled.

"But, Mister—"

"Not going to tell you again—get *down*!" he blustered.

Grabbing Sari by the arm, Junie sputtered, "The voice is talking, Sari, but he not listening," he said, pointing at Zachary.

This time, Sari popped up. "You gotta listen, Zachary. The voice never wrong."

Junie spoke up. "Turn up ahead. Yes, now make a sharp left here. Go into that lot. Get between them other trucks that look like this one."

"It's a shuttle," Zachary said as he pulled right where he was directed.

And as though an invisible shield went over them, they watched from the lot as Legend continued flying up the street, following the wrong shuttle. Finally, mixing it up with the tourists, the four got out of the shuttle and made it to the back of the visitor's lot.

Lifting his duffle, Zachary took a tool out of it and popped the door of the conversion van.

"No other way?" John asked.

"No other way," Zachary said, and they all climbed in. "I don't like stealing, but I hate dying worse. And I know the man after us. He will not hesitate to put a bullet right between my eyes. So, please, spare me the wrong or the right of it. We got a two-day trip to get to the Rocky Mountains in Colorado."

"Whoop!" Junie laughed. "He said Colorado, y'all, and Colorado it is."

"Who's he?" Zachary wanted to know. "And are you talking to him on the phone? We'll have to get rid of it if you are."

John looked around the van, then walked to the back, where he lay down. Everyone could see his eyes were red, and he was tired.

Sari moved up front and sat in the seat next to Zachary. "Junie hears from Heaven. Papa says it's an angel. Mama said it was God. But what we all agree is, it's divine, and he's never let us down."

"Uh, Sari, I don't know if I believe that."

Her eyes widened, and Sari gasped. "I never met anyone who didn't believe. Where I'm from, we all had to believe in something. Some folks kept the old ways and prayed to what Mama said was idols. But life was too hard not to believe in something." She sighed. "Life been easy for you, Zachary?"

"No, it hasn't. And maybe since this has all begun, I feel a little different. But voices? Come on, now."

Junie sniffed as if offended. "Mr. Zachary, you just saw the voice at work, and you deny the power therein?"

The van got quiet, and they waited for Zachary to respond. Instead, he cut on the radio and said, "This is a radio. It plays all kinds of music. You can listen and learn. Junie, hand me your phone, so I can put it on this charger they have plugged in up here."

Handing it over, Junie watched him plug it in. He then went to the back and called up front, "What are these little screens back here?"

"Must be video screens. Some people have them to keep occupied on long trips. Look on the floor and see if you see any square discs with pictures on them."

Junie saw a box and opened it. Inside were several movies on compact discs. Pulling one out with slaves on the cover, John shook his head.

"But, Papa, don't you want to know what they thought our lives were like back then?"

"Don't care," John said belligerently. Then looking contrite, he said, "Sorry, Junie. I'm tired down to the soles of my feet."

"You go on and sleep, Papa. I'll just watch a little of it," Junie said, taking the *Roots* CD out of the case.

"Push that button that says 'Out' on the black box on the floor, and if there is a disc there, take it out. Then put yours in, hit 'In,' and it will start."

When the music began to play, Zachary turned their radio down when Sari went to the back to look. "It's like yesterday on the phone but bigger," she said.

"There are screens way bigger than that, bigger than this van," Zachary said.

They watched as the man held the baby up to the sky in technicolor.

Junie stared in reverence at the father-and-son moment. He then turned to his father. "Papa, did you hold me up to the sky?"

John had an eye open, watching the screen, when he solemnly said, "No, son, the sky would always cover you. I held you to my chest, less one day, you be taken from me."

Chapter Twenty-Seven

The road was asphalt and potholed, and the motel didn't look inviting, but they had dumped the van after driving for around five hours. They left it deep inside a junkyard site in Charleston, West Virginia. They then picked up another car with Zachary's five-finger discount and drove until they made it to Louisville, Kentucky. This no-tell motel was on its outskirts.

Zachary went in, head and face covered, and paid with cash for a room in the back on the other side of the motel. He then parked the SUV four doors down, and they all entered their room.

"I'll sleep on the floor. Junie, you and Sari sleep together. Zachary, you must be flat-out tired. You can have the other bed," John said, adding, "Good thing I got plenty of rest in before we changed cars. I thank ya."

Zachary stared at Sari with longing, and she returned the look. "Night, sweetheart," he said.

"Night, darling," Junie answered and then fell out chuckling. "I declare, you two mooning around like two sick calves at branding time."

"Dats all dey better be doing," John snarled. Then holding up his hand to Junie, he groaned. "And I know, Junie, *enunciate*."

Junie lay down next to his sister, who lay down while keeping her eyes on Zachary. He did the same.

"I'm not putting up with this all night," Junie said as he got up and went around and lay between the two, cutting off their vision. "Now, please, go to sleep."

"Junie, you forget *I'm* the older sister, *little* brother. You get back where you were. *I'm* in charge, *not* you," she said in a stern, hushed voice.

"In charge? How are you in charge when you bark on command? Roll over on command? But unlike any other good pet, you rarely bite."

Gasping, Sari whimpered in embarrassment. "I fought, Junie. And Missus didn't tell me to bark. You made that up. Now, take it back."

"Woof, woof!" Junie said.

"You through, Junie?" John said quietly.

Gulping, Junie's voice cracked. "Sorry, Papa."

"Sorry can't close the gate on the heaping of hurt you just threw on your sistah. 'Sorry' just make it possible to shake the dirt offa your feet while you keep moving forward, and the hurt chain *her* down. You know about chaining a soul, Junie?"

Sari cried as she bit her lip and snot ran down her pinched, drenched face. She turned away, her hunched, heaving shoulders giving her back to everyone.

Zachary rose, but John shook his head for him to back down.

John sat next to her on her side of the bed and patted her back. "We all under a lot of pressure. Your brother has especially been struggling without his angel. Now, he's back. He understands even more, hearing his angel is a gift *and* a responsibility."

Junie flipped over in the bed and looked at his sister. "I'se awful remorseful, Sari girl. My mouth left the stall before the stallion had a rider. Sure way for a crash to happen. My apologies."

Sari wiped her eyes. "You said 'I'se,' Junie."

"Yeah, I know. I got a little bit stirred up. I'm sorry, sis. I'll move."

"Nope. Stay right where you at. This way, me and Zachary will continue to get along just fine. I don't want to have to count the many reasons I have to hurt him. I never count past three," John said.

Zachary, who watched the family dynamics and heard the veiled threat, sat down and turned over in his bed. "Well, on that note, good night."

The early-morning room was coal-black dark when Zachary heard the toilet flush. Realizing due to his exhaustion, he had not opened the door and showed everyone where the bathroom was, he paused to see who had come out. He was glad he showed them how a toilet worked earlier in the day when they first stopped for gas. It was an embarrassing but necessary chore because the Bensons didn't have a frame of reference for modern hygiene. Sari averted her eyes the whole time he spoke, and her cheeks bloomed a peachy amber hue against the high yellow of her skin tone. Junie then compounded the issue with a young boy's usual aplomb on all things awkward when, with a scrunched-up nose, he shared that the Boiler Room had them going in chamber pots.

Zachary knew hell was waiting for Edgar Burstein, and he would bust it wide open.

Midyawn, the door creaked open, and the light over the sink outlined a slender silhouette. Entranced, Zachary soaked in her beauty. His mind strummed a telepathic message.

Can I touch you . . . please?

As Sari began to tiptoe around his bed, he reached out and touched her hand ever so lightly. He didn't think she felt it but soon realized he was mistaken. She returned the tenderness of his touch when she used her finger and adjusted the flop of brownish blond hair in disarray around his face. He noted her rapt expression in awe as the small streams of light bathed her face.

Angelic.

He knew this woman and had spent years with her in his dreams. He had built castles for her and slew dragons, and now, she was here in the flesh. He held his breath as she bent over and pressed her lips to his. It was innocent in its delivery. No open mouth or wailing tongue. But it was the sweetest, most phenomenal kiss of his life. It spoke to tomorrow. It spoke to long nights in front of a fire. It spoke of growing old together as they celebrated anniversaries and children's birthdays.

Looking over at her father, his body still in the dark, she touched her hand to her lips. Sari softly breathed, "Good night, sweetheart."

Ready to answer her with the desires of his heart, his vision expanded past her body. He saw the muscled form of her father. John's piercing gaze was laser pointed on his as he raised his head from the floor and mouthed to Zachary, *"That's one."*

Chapter Twenty-Eight

After showers that challenged the pressure of the motel's plumbing system, the group got back on the road in early dawn. After another full day of driving and fast food, the fascination with videos and XM radio was over for all three of the Bensons. They were glad that what would have taken a month now took only two days. But the manufactured air and the constant motion were wearing. They wanted out so they could figure out what their lives would look like starting tomorrow.

Humming to herself, Sari sat next to Zachary as she asked a million questions about him and life in the new millennium.

"You enjoyed being a soldier? Killing folk?" Sari said, her voice strained in disbelief.

"No, not killing people; *saving* people. I went into the war to defend my country," Zachary stressed.

"Before we run, Lincoln was going to run for president, and people were fit to be tied. Us slaves went to bed with hope in our hearts. But the plantation owners, the reverend, all of them free people told us how horrible freedom would be, told us we would starve, be homeless, that our owners were taking care of us, and we needed them."

Zachary listened but also needed her to understand he was not a killer. "I understand, and that was horrible, but—"

Sari's voice was strained as she seemed to reach for the right words. "Uh-uh. They said we was lazy, but we built the house, cooked, cleaned it, and brought the money into it *they* lived on. Said they had a right to it because this country said so. Slavery still be, if someone had not said no, suh. Ain't that so, Zachary?" she said, crossing her arms, her mouth in a scowl.

Zachary couldn't argue what he had not endured. He could only hope she heard his truth. "Sarah, I wish I could turn back the hands of time and stop what happened to you and all those who look like you. I went into the army to defend democracy and to defend those who couldn't defend themselves. Our country has this wonderful Declaration of Independence that our governing body rarely lives by. But I stood shoulder to shoulder with others who thought like me and wanted to fight for the greater good. And now *you're* my greater good."

Zachary could see her facial features thawing from her brow line to the slow grin that spread across her face. "You too sweet, Zachary."

Hearing her Southern magnolia drawl made Zachary look back to see they were not being overheard. He then whispered, "I'm sweet on you. I already have a Sarah ache. I want you to know I'll never get enough of you."

Feeling warm breath on his neck, Zachary looked up at his mirror, expecting to see Junie hanging on the back of his seat. Instead, hard eyes beaded on him, and then John mouthed, "*That's two.*"

Zachary pulled his T-shirt collar away from his now-sweating body . . . and then their SUV was slammed from behind.

Gripping the steering wheel, Zachary yelled, "Grab your seat belts and strap in."

"Is somebody doing a poor job of passing us?" Junie yelled.

"No! They've found us," Zachary said as he maneuvered. "I didn't want to say anything, but we're only ten miles away from our destination. If we made it there, we would be impenetrable. It's a compound of retired and disabled Special Forces. No one would *dare* attack it."

"Have they been following us the whole time?" John said as he looked down at the knives strapped to his upper thigh. He then looked for any other weapon he could use. Seeing a toolbox, he opened it and put the hammer through his belt loop.

"No. Legend must have found the car I dumped in West Virginia. I should have never parked it in that person's garage. He's been one step ahead of us. This compound we're going to is known only to those with an invite. Somehow, Legend must know about it. I was assured he was never invited. As an ex-Special Forces, he knew to wait for us on this narrow path and cut us off before we got there. Hold tight! I'm going to swing into this grove of trees. When I do, everyone pile out and run."

"I'm not leaving you!" Sari screamed, "Papa, tell him. We'll help him fight!"

John squeezed Sari's shoulder. "Sari girl, get out of your seat and come back here with your brother. When he stops, you and Junie run like the dickens. I'll stay with Zachary."

Nodding but not saying a word, Zachary handed John a gun. "Just like I showed you when we went out for food. Aim, then squeeze the trigger. This baby has enough rounds to keep them busy. Then use the knives I gave you. You still strapped?"

"Yeah, I'm good with knives too. I got you. I'll not be in your way."

Slamming the car between two tight trees, he screamed, "Now now now!"

Feet bounded out the back door and took off into the woods. Gunshots battered the SUV as Zachary and John hid behind trees and fired back. But as many as they took down, the senator had enough money for new ones to take their place. They were being swarmed.

Tree bark flew in Zachary's face as he saw John fighting hand-to-hand combat with a man. One blow with his hammer, and the man went down. But before John could regroup, another took his place, slicing him in his upper arm.

Grabbing his assailant by the neck, John broke it with his mighty strength and pivoted to the next. He threw him over his back and then was fighting two more. But like cockroaches in the night, they kept swarming.

Zachary tried, but he couldn't get to John. He was pinned down and had switched guns when the other ran out of ammo. Every time he tried to get from behind the tree to help John, a volley of bullets pinned him back. In the background, he could tell the location of Sari and Junie by her screams and his sobs. He tried to call out that she was giving away her location and that she should run, but she couldn't hear him over her own screams and his bullets.

Frustrated, he saw Legend's men fanning out to go around him and get to Sari and Junie. He looked over and couldn't see John. He had one last chance.

"Legend! Hear me out, man," Zachary bellowed. "They're innocent—caught up in a freak accident that they happened to live through. Don't do this, man."

"Stand down, boy. You're outnumbered and outgunned. I don't want to do this. Don't make me. Whatever the senator does, it won't be as bad as what Burstein Labs had planned. I'll give you to the count of three."

Why is everyone giving me to the count of three?

"I'm not giving them to you," Zachary yelled back.

"Then I'll take them."

Zachary then saw Legend motion with his hand in the air in a circle. He knew they were moving in, and he had one desperate play in him. Stepping out from behind the tree, Zachary gave a heroic war cry and splattered the front of him in a wide arc, dropping men like flies.

"Run!" Zachary screamed as his words merged into a gurgle, and he fell to the ground, two bullets felling him.

Barely breathing, Zachary could hear Sari and Junie's hysterical screaming and sobbing. Then seeing their feet dragged by him, a pair of combat boots loomed over him.

"I'll send your lovely wife, Sylvia, flowers now that I've made her a widow."

A feral scream pierced the air as Sari fought like a tigress for the men to let her go. "You lie. You lie," she wailed to Zachary. "Papa, Papa," she cried.

As she was slammed over a soldier's shoulder and carried to the black van, Junie was dragged behind her as he looked all over the foliage for his father, to no avail. Silent tears coursed down his face and dripped from his chin as steel formed in his dark brown eyes.

A small puff of air escaped Zachary's mouth, and his heart cracked open before everything went black.

Chapter Twenty-Nine

Sari stood at the bay window in a beautiful vintage taffeta pale-blue gown. Her auburn-tipped wiry curls had been tamed into a chignon, and her hands had been scrubbed and paraffin dipped to softness. Her nails were shaped, trimmed, and shined with a French manicure, and her makeup was subtle but illuminating. She appeared a picture-perfect pampered princess, but her eyes were vacant . . . joyless.

Married, married, and never once stopped to tell me the truth. He wasn't free to love me.

"You still staring out that window, Sari girl? Still just a lot of acres filled with trees. It look like it used to look, only minus the slaves."

Turning toward her brother, she asked the question she asked him every day, "What does your angel say, Junie?"

"He don't say anything about running, Sari. I just keep getting nudged to the library, where Senator Benson lets me read whatever I want. I keep reading law books, though, and it's taking forever to know why. I read a paragraph, and then I have to look up most of the words I'm reading. It's really very taxing."

"Junie, do you really think Papa's gone? I've cried so many tears, but he don't feel gone in here," she said as she placed her hand over her heart.

He sat next to her on the couch she had moved to. "I try not to think about it. Every time I've imagined our freedom, Papa was there, and now, well, he's not, and I can't rightly bring myself to it. So, I pretend it hasn't happened."

"We forget you're smart as any man but still only twelve years old."

"We never got to be children. I should have a birthday coming up. But then I'm what, one hundred seventy-five? I see these shows on television and see twelve-year-olds, and I can't marvel at the freedom their childhood gives them. Where is the senator, Sari?"

"Don't know. Don't care. We been here two weeks, and he say he has something to tell both of us today. He had them put me in this fancy gown, and I see you in a stylish suit. So, we wait and brace ourselves."

A clatter sounded at the door, then the senator entered with a mahogany-carved wooden cane, his seafoam eyes cold and hair of silver. He was regal in his posture and had an air of superiority inbred in those who were rarely told no.

"No need to be alarmed. This is good news." The senator walked into the room with a stack of leather-bound journals in his arms. Beside him matching his progress was his assistant, Grover, who carried a large, covered, framed painting in his slender hands.

Sitting forward, Junie and Sari pensively waited. Finally, the senator pulled his chair in front of them and placed the journals on the cocktail table. He then tapped his cane on the floor.

"I can't begin to tell you how exciting this all has become." Stroking the journals with reverence, he exclaimed with delight, "You were a young boy's impossible image to aspire to, Junie. Reading about your decisions on stocks and your irrigation systems that were later expanded on and patented by others . . ." He stood and strolled to the window. Then pointing outside, he said. "It's all still here because of you, my dear boy—and here you are!"

Folding his arms and refusing to play dumb, Junie glared at the senator. "Yet, my family and I have nothing to show for our labor. And you have everything."

"Nothing to show? Look around you. Where is your satisfaction in producing a legacy that has stayed the hands of time for over one hundred and sixty years? Surely, you understand your role in the scheme of things. You were born to serve, boy."

Eyes glazed with malice, Junie growled from deep in his throat. A softened hand circled his wrist when he would have leaped and attacked. "Patience, Junie," she murmured, refusing to blink first as she held the senator's stare.

His green eyes twinkled as though Junie's ire was too minuscule even to consider a danger. "And you, my dear. So beautiful. I could see why he loathed to give you to the highest bidder. But finally, a bid came in for you that was so much money. Even your father couldn't turn it down."

Dirty, Sari's throat tightened as she hollered, "No more lies. My papa would never—"

A blur sailed over Sari as Junie finally leaped on top of the senator, pummeling him with his fists, landing blows on his face and chest before his assistant could pull Junie away. Then the door bang opened, and Legend entered, gun drawn.

Holding a squirming Junie and approaching a stricken Sari, his assistant drawled, "Shall I remove the trash, sir?"

Straightening his suit and patting his bloodied mouth with a handkerchief, the senator looked at the tiny droplets of blood that clung to the silk fabric square. "No, the boy needs to understand his place here . . . and his sister's."

"Very well, Senator," his assistant said as he dragged a struggling Junie over to a chair farther away from them. Legend then moved and stood next to Junie's chair.

"What is *my* place, then. Please, enlighten me," Sari said.

Motioning for his assistant to bring the painting forward, the senator bent down and removed the covering. In the picture, a woman, blond hair flowing into a chignon with loose tendrils framing Sari's face, sat in the very dress that Sari sat wearing today.

A gasp escaped Sari's mouth as she perused the picture, her head shaking as she tried to stammer out her thoughts. "It . . . can't . . . no!" Her hand then covered her mouth so that she stopped the words that regurgitated from her mouth in horror.

Throwing his head back, the senator cackled his pleasure. "You are the spitting image of my great-aunt Lucinda. Imagine my surprise when I thought I was after what was stolen from the fracking site, only to discover what was stolen more than a hundred and sixty years before."

His laughter stopped, and his stare went vacant as he said in a sinister fashion, "No one steals from a Benson—ever." Then snapping out of his trance, he continued. "But I digress, my dear. You are my many times removed . . . aunt!"

Picking up the journal, he continued, "It's all right here. The many nights of satisfaction my ancestor enjoyed from the touch of your mother. How her mind and words called him out of his own wife's bed to hers time and time again. His final decision to leave her alone as he was losing himself over to her charms and was even considering freeing her. Instead, he gave her to your precious papa to wed."

"Nooooooo!" Sari said and collapsed onto the settee.

Junie fought with all he had to go to her but was kept captured by Legend's brutal strength. There would be bruises to show for Junie's gallant effort to protect his sister.

"Let the boy go, Legend. It must be a shock to learn his sister is really his half sister, my great-great-great-great-grandfather's bastard mulatto."

"Junie," she cried as he ran to her and held her to his smaller frame.

"It don't matter none, Sari girl. I'm *still* your brother; Papa still your papa. Only Papa you know. Don't matter none."

Sniffling, Sari closed her eyes, and as if dawn came on a new morning, she rose with the grace of a fresh beginning. "It is unseemly for a person of status to crow about a crime, Senator. And rape *is* a crime. I have listened to your talk shows and watched your television shows, and if I remember correctly, forcing someone against their will *is* a crime—as it should be. Your ancestor was a rapist, sir."

Raising his cane as though to strike her down, he stopped mid-stroke. He then nodded, and his assistant took the oil painting and replaced it on the wall where it had earlier been removed.

"I was never able to have children. I have a sappy, mewling nephew and a many-times-divorced niece who can't keep her legs closed, both of whom I despise, that will inherit this place. But I see the Benson intelligence shining through your eyes, even if it's in that disgusting melanin-shaded face. In two more generations, that melanin skin will be wiped clean. I plan to breed you as my ancestors had planned. But this time, for a child that will be mine. I will ensure that child will marry well and *that* grandchild will inherit all." Walking around Sari, his cane hitting the hardened floor, he said, "An accident at sixteen years old on a horse gave me this bum leg and made me sterile. I'm forty-eight years old and have longed for a child. This will all work out nicely."

"And if I will not submit to your lunacy?" an incredulous Sari asked.

"Oh, you'll submit." Then an inscrutable look passed between him and his assistant. "Even if you don't enjoy it. I have handpicked your possible baby's daddy."

Legend then walked over and scooped Sari into his arms.

"Take her to her room and have your men stand guard while she gets used to the idea of her new circumstances," the senator instructed. Then seeing her stricken face, he added, "Her little brother is allowed to visit, but post men below the window too."

After they left the room, the senator's focus shifted to Junie. "You struck me, boy. In another time, that would have meant death. Shoot, in this time, it could still be carried out. But I'm a man of vision, and you can do for me what you once did for my ancestors. Now, you need some more formal education. I've arranged for a professor to instruct you in today's economics and other needed subjects." Turning to leave the room, he then paused. "And to ensure you understand your situation," he ticked off his fingers, "this plantation is over three hundred acres large. You are in a world where you don't exist, and the two people who tried to help you are dead. Where you going to go?" Seeing Junie's despondency, he cajoled. "But I'm a benevolent benefactor, and you may have full use of the house, including the library of movies and video games when you're not studying."

Reaching the door, he said to his assistant, "Let the professor know he has two months before I expect this investment to be ready to start paying his own way. Remember, they can be a lazy people. So make sure he keeps him on track. And only give him thirty minutes a day of free time. I'm not *that* benevolent." He chuckled as they both left the room.

Junie sat listening to the nudges of the voice, assuring him he was not alone. He could still feel his papa's presence in this life.

Where are you, Papa?

Chapter Thirty

Feeling the bandage and his taped chest, Zachary pulled his arm gingerly back and forth, opening and shutting his hand, flexing each finger. Over and over, he performed this ritual as he inhaled and exhaled with each movement.

"How's he doing?" Zachary asked as his old platoon leader, Malachi, clicked into the room on his titanium-built artificial legs.

"He's sore and grumbling to get going to find his kids. Can't say I blame him. The man is built like a redwood tree. His gunshot flesh wound is healing and has progressed much faster than yours. It's his concussion that was the problem. He hit his head against the car door when he fell, and that's what kept him down." Then answering an earlier request from Zachary, he said, "Checked back, and it looks like no one has seen Edgar Burstein since the mysterious burning down of his lab. I did check on your people, and they all got out alive. Looks like Legend's men used nonlethal force when engaging them. They all are scared enough not to talk. According to the news, no one saw or heard anything."

Zachary sang, "Have you ever seen such a sight in your life as three blind mice?" Then he groaned, "Of mice and men, my friend, courage is a rare commodity."

"And you know this," Malachi answered in comedian Chris Tucker's voice. "And by the way, John still refuses to see you. Said something about when he does see you, that's three. So what'd you do to him except help him escape?"

"Long story short, I fell in love with his daughter while technically still married to Sylvia."

Covering his mouth with his hand to stop his chortle, Malachi said, "You don't do easy. How do you fall in love with someone in seventy-two hours? Especially someone who is from another time? Man, me and all the crew are still wrapping our minds around *that* one."

"Me too. Just know I've had a connection to her for a long time. We both just finally caught up to what had been forming for years. That's *if* I can get her to talk to me now." Standing, he said, "It's been two weeks. I need to get going soon. I agree with John. We have to go save them. And I need to apologize to my future before it's etched into my past."

"Yeah, well, ugly want to be pretty, but that don't make the image in the mirror change. You got to heal, especially if you want to go against Legend. He's a beast, and we both know it. Pretty mutha—"

"—Humph, I'll be ready. There was just something in my mind that told me he wouldn't end me. But by God, the sucker shot me point-blank."

"Uh, yeah. How 'bout *twice*? If it's any consolation to you, they weren't kill shots, which means he didn't intend to kill you. And someone reporting on our radio that shots were fired in our vicinity sent us out looking. We found you ten miles out. So I'd say he did you a solid."

"That's what *you* say. A solid would have been to leave me standing, or better yet, letting me go on my way. But you can't expect integrity from a priest in a whorehouse."

Laughing with gusto, Malachi said, "I missed you, man. Last few times I spoke to you, that crazy wit was missing."

"My ex-wife was holding it hostage." Sighing, he added, "My attorney says she's holding her ground on signing the papers. I told him to tell her I'd give her the house if she would sign now. That house cost me half a mil to please her. I'm waiting on her answer. Man, I *need* to be divorced."

"I'd say another week of rehab, and you guys will be ready. I have four men who have voluntold to go with you. Don't make me regret twisting their arms. They survived one war. I don't want them to come home on their own soil in body bags."

"*I* helped you make it home, didn't I?" Zachary said, then looking at Malachi's missing legs, he rephrased his words, "Well, *most* of you."

"You ever had your butt kicked by a man with no legs? 'Cause it's coming."

"Roger that, Lieutenant." He saluted. "I gotta say thanks for all you've done for me and for the place here. It's amazing."

Malachi crossed his arms and leaned against the wall. "I came home to nothing, guy. Girl left me. No parents left. PTSD where I'm screaming into sweaty nights of terror. And all around me were other veterans with similar histories. So I thought, what-if?"

"You did more than think what-if."

"Not at first. It was all daydreams, and then in the VA Hospital, I heard rumors. There are right-wing groups in there trolling for new members. I was despondent, then pissed, then energized to do something different. Where were the paramilitary groups that would be ready to fight these groups instigating hate?"

Zachary frowned. "Wait. You never shared this—"

"—You and most like you can't wrap your mind around the darkness of some of these folk whipped up by the dark web and small-minded creeps in dark rooms, spinning webs of deceit. Can't understand why you aren't better at work? Gotta be the Black man they hired. Lost your man? Had to be the sultry, slutty moves of the Latina woman he's now dating. Minorities are the world's answers to every problem they have."

"Wow . . . I can't say I would have understood before Sarah, but, man, I sure get it now."

"They say love illuminates."

Zachary smirked. "And now, you're here and growing. And you have mad-skilled people joining you. As many white, as black, as Latino."

"We're three hundred strong, now. I think we are the true army of tomorrow. And I think we are who God has chosen to win."

"Man, it's going to take me a minute to wrap my mind about what you are versus what I *thought* you were," Zachary ruminated.

Malachi slapped his shoulder as he moved to leave. "As you were. I'm out of here."

Deciding that he needed to get out of his pity party, Zachary launched forward with his hands out in front of him. He attempted to lower himself into a squat but teetered over.

Darn it!

Malachi solemnly looked back and quietly shut the door.

Two Weeks Later . . .

"One week more, my butt," Zachary swore as he stood on the porch of the small cabin and watched John sprint across the grounds, racing two other men. "He's fast," Zachary said, gesturing at John's form.

"Faster than last week. He gets faster, stronger, and more irritated by the day. Knocked Cole clean out during his martial arts drill. Seems he was already trained in Dambe, an African form of fighting."

"He'll be ready to leave tomorrow. But before we go, he and I have to have a meeting of the minds. I can't be watching my back *and* my front out there."

Malachi's tongue rolled a toothpick around in his mouth. "We just got both of you patched up. Don't make us have to do it all over again." Then lifting his fist, he said, "Give solidarity a chance."

Zachary returned it with a peace sign. "It won't be me. That man is going to be my father-in-law. I must find a way to make him understand my actions."

Malachi said, "Good luck with that because *I* don't understand your actions."

Stepping down from the porch, Zachary met John as he returned to his cabin. The other men moved back out of the way as the two men circled each other.

"If you'll let me explain—"

"—three!" John roared as he swung and hit Zachary on the chin so hard he went down. "Get up, you sorry snake."

Rubbing his chin, Zachary stayed down. "I think I can talk to you from here. You're not the kind of person that would hit me while I'm down." John lurched at him, and Zachary protected his face. Then when no blow came, he peeped.

"I owed you that for leading my Sari on. I've had nothing but trouble from white folk. I try to remember my friend, Donald, who helped us escape. But the rest of you haven't given me much hope. Then I met you. Took me a minute to wrap my head around you being her choice. But I accepted it. Then you turn out to be a snake. You cut the heads off snakes, mister."

"I'm not a snake. I love your daughter, and I'm in the process of getting a divorce." Getting to his knees, Zachary looked up. "There are only two people that understand. I've known Sari through my dreams since I was a young boy. She's been my idea that I thought would never be real. Now she is. I don't expect you to understand it, but I can't . . . no—I *won't* give her up."

"You hurt her," John said.

"And in hurting her, I hurt me," Zachary said and rose. "The only way I can begin to make it up to her is to go and get her and explain it myself."

Turning and walking away, John stopped and pivoted back to Zachary. "I'll see you in the morning."

Zachary watched as John stormed into his cabin. *Well, that went well.*

Meeting in the morning, the six men loaded their supplies in two all-terrain vehicles and rolled out. Malachi had provided some intel that the senator's tourist attraction, Benson Plantation, was closed for the season. Their marketing team had put out a statement to the public that they were closed for repairs, but no construction trucks were noted. However, the plantation did have an increase in security around its perimeter. Sealing the validity of the intel was Legend's constant presence going in and out of the guarded gate. As such, the group's destination was evident.

"It's been four weeks since I last saw my children," John lamented from the passenger seat next to Zachary. "We've never been separated before." He paused. "That's a miracle, really, because most of us was missing our kinfolk in them days. It be a cursed life."

Zachary didn't know how to respond to that. His hands at the wheel, he saw the sun peeking over the mountain as they made their way to Tennessee. They could have flown in and found transportation when they got there, but faster wasn't always better. They had made it out of the compound through a hidden exit in the woods where the two vehicles were stashed and covered and would get there without anyone knowing they were coming.

John studied the terrain and said in wonder, "This car moves so fast. I wonder if you know how amazing this is. We're going to be there in twenty hours, and when we escaped, it took a month of inching forward in a wagon." Shivering, he rubbed his arms. "Neva been so scared in my life. Scared I fail, and we'd get forced back, separated. Now, here we are, and I failed, and we separated."

His look was so forlorn that Zachary searched for words that would help him feel less guilt, less shame. "You got them further than most. I don't know a lot, but I've read about what happens when a slave who runs gets caught. Man, you ran so hard that you ran right into one hundred sixty years in the future."

"Ha! Only to be captured in a time that man's not being enslaved anymore," John said with chagrin. "Yet, here we are."

"There are all kinds of ways people are enslaved, even today," Zachary said, thinking of the marriage he despised and the job he had stayed on that he hated. "It's not the same by any means, but all chains chafe."

"I appreciate you helping me get my children back. Can't promise it will end well for you and Sari. She's a stubborn little thing; always has been. But I'll say thank you now before I close my eyes and get some rest. 'Cause come Benson Plantation, there won't be no rest for the weary, and hell gon' receive some new souls."

Surprised by John's candor, Zachary saw him place his baseball cap on his face and slide down in his seat. Snores continued to filter in the air from the backseat, and Zachary, who loved to think and drive, leaned back and let the road meet them.

Later that night . . .

On silent feet, the men spread out. They already had intel from scouts sent out a week before on changing of the guards and Legend's weak points along the parameter. The wrought iron fence with spiked tops held the lassoed rope well as they climbed over it.

Looking over at John, Zachary grimaced as he pulled himself over and watched John seem to scale the fence effortlessly. The drills the guys had done with him demonstrated that the fit thirty-eight-year-old would have been a natural for the armed forces in another life.

Running behind a tree, Zachary physically shook off his thoughts of age. Whenever he tried to figure out Sari being twenty, but really over a hundred years old, and John only six years older than him—but not really—his head was on the verge of exploding. If he added Junie to the mix, the puzzle became epic size—and he gave up. He then accepted what he had always heard: age is nothing but a number. And he had never been good at math.

Chapter Thirty-One

Junie knocked on Sari's door as the guard stood aside under the orders that Junie could come and go as he wanted.

"Come in."

Walking into the room in sneakers, blue jeans, and the T-shirt they arrived in, Junie went straight to Sari's closet. "Here," he said, throwing a pair of tennis shoes at her from deep inside the closet. Then bending down and rummaging in a basket, he pulled out jeans and threw them out to her next. "Put these on."

Taking the wrinkled jeans, she put them to her nose and smelled them. "Uh-uh, Junie. They stink."

"That is because you wouldn't let Clara wash them. So, put them on, and the shoes. I have no idea what is happening, but the urge to be ready is pushing something fierce in my chest," Junie said as he rubbed his chest in an up-and-down pattern.

Sari shook out the jeans and slid them on under her T-shirt sleep shirt. She then put on the shoes and went over to her window. Pulling back the curtain slightly at the corner, she watched as the guard stood right under her window. "He's still there," she whispered.

Junie exchanged places with her and then looked back and forth. "Where? I don't see anyone."

Moving him aside, Sari looked again. Then animated, she said, "He's gone. Junie, is this it? Will we finally get out of this place? I can't take one more Ivy League scholar being pranced in front of me like a brooding buck. I swear you can smell the heat coming off them."

"Just be glad he has decided to try to woo you to his way of thinking. It's given me some time to research how things work. I think that we have a chance, and I think it's why we were brought to this time period. God will not be mocked, Sari."

Two quick knocks came on their door. When it was swung open, standing on the other side . . . was John, and at his feet was their guard.

Sari and Junie ran to him, already half-sobbing, "Papa."

"Children," he said, grabbing and pulling them out the door as he gathered them to him. "Glad to see you, but we gotta move."

All of them ran down the stairs as Zachary stood watch at the front door. Bodies lay along the way, with darts protruding out of different parts of their flesh. Zachary looked up, and the instant he and Sari's eyes connected, the room stopped, and everything else faded into the background. He touched his heart, letting her know she owned it.

Suddenly, the door was flung against its hinges, and Legend stood with a gun slung over his shoulder and one on his hip. The one in his hand was pointed directly at Sari. "Nobody move."

Sporting a large grin, he said to Zachary, "I always wanted to say that ever since Clint Eastwood said, 'Make my day.'"

"Not funny," Zachary said.

"No, but let me tell you what *is* hilarious. For old times' sake, I left my friend alive, hoping he would take the hint and live another day. Then I watched and waited, and lo and behold, his hero tendencies did not let me down. Here he is in my neck of the woods, begging me to finish the job."

"This is beyond you, Legend. And I also held back for what was once a friendship. You wanted to know who was the best? So put down your gear and let's get to it," Zachary said as he disarmed himself and waved for everyone to move out of the way. "Just space and consequences."

John moved Sari and Junie behind him and nodded for Zachary to finish it.

Legend spat on the floor and threw down his gear. Then pulling out a knife, he began to circle Zachary, taunting him. "Didn't know you was into some old stuff. I mean, what is she, one hundred eighty years old? Well preserved, but, man, how 'bout them cobwebs?"

Zachary lunged forward when Sari screeched her ire, and Legend sliced his arm. "There you go, getting all emotional. You had that fine, lily-white orchid of the valley, Sylvia, and here you are pulling up African violets. Tut, tut, man. Sad."

Zachary lunged again and was sliced across the opposite arm.

Legend boomed, "You making this too easy. Senator trying to breed her with the best, so he can have her sire him the perfect son. Then, raise him to sire another child who'll become the perfect white heir for all of this. He'll breed the nigra right out of her offspring. Shoot, I'm good-looking, smart, and rich. Maybe I'll get in line too. What do you think?" he said, as he swiped at Zachary, missed, and then was punched in the chest by Zachary.

"You talk too much," Zachary said, both arms dripping with blood as he did a roundhouse kick and caught Legend in the shoulder. When Legend spun, Zachary caught him with a right hook and then punched him in the throat. Gurgling, Legend fell to his knees. Zachary bent over and hit him as hard as he could across the head, hoping to knock him out for hours.

John grabbed both his children's hands and began dragging them out the door.

"*Wait!*" Junie yelled and ran into the library. Going behind a desk, he moved the rug, put a combination into the safe door, and opened it. He then reached inside and pulled out the journals. Grabbing the pile, he handed some back to his father and Sari. Then standing, he yelled, "Now, we can go."

They all jumped into one vehicle, and the other four men followed behind them as they passed bodies littered throughout the grounds with darts sticking out of their unconscious bodies.

Zachary, who was next to Sari, held her hand tentatively. "I'm sorry. I promise you that I was already in the process of getting a divorce. I just didn't have a chance or privacy to explain everything to you. I signed the papers yesterday. I am free to court you properly with permission from your father. I want you to meet my family. My mother and father, and my sisters and brothers."

Covering her mouth with her hand, Sari sat in stunned silence. She then said, "Where could we live? Where would they let us be?"

"We're going to fix that right now," Zachary said as they sped through the streets. "You ever heard of the eleven o'clock news?"

Chapter Thirty-Two

The news anchor spun in his chair as the camera swung back to him from a news clip from the night the Bensons were rescued. "And there you have it told to you from the people who lived it. People who lived in the pre–Civil War era, escaped from slavery, only to be frozen in time . . . and then enslaved again."

The redheaded female newscaster's blue eyes dripped with tears. "To hear their story straight from their own mouths . . . To get firsthand accounts of the hardship of daily life during that time, only to have our own Senator Benson be impeached from his position and, in shame, take his own life. This has been two months of a media circus. Maybe we can let these poor people rest now."

The other senior newscaster with silver at his temples looked deep into the camera. "America and the rest of the world have watched this play out in every medium possible. We have heard from psychologists, historians, politicians, and legal experts who have given their perspectives on the lawsuits filed by John, Sarah, and Junie Benson. The plantation journals were authenticated from that era, proving Junie Benson was instrumental in providing the wealth the plantation was built on. Sari Benson's DNA provided further proof that she is a direct descendent—Jacob Benson's daughter—chronicled in his journals. And now, the last part of the puzzle—the lawsuit for false imprisonment, asking for all rights to the land and all it entails, as well as reparations for work completed but never compensated."

After a pregnant pause, the television screen switched to the courthouse's front steps. There, a female correspondent, her head covered in a hijab, reported, "The Senate has had a field day with the ramifications of what this could mean to so many families who can trace their ancestry back to today's wealth. A closed courtroom, with no cameras or media in the room, has had all of us panting in anticipation. And so we wait, some in fear, others in desperation." Then suddenly, behind her, the courthouse doors opened.

"Wait, wait. The jury must have returned because people are starting to come out. We will soon learn the results of the lawsuit."

The camera zoomed in on the scene of the courthouse steps. A distinguished team of lawyers stood at the top of the steps to make an official statement and answer questions. People poured in front of them, some screaming, some solemn.

A gopher hurriedly placed a podium and microphone in front of them. Then a well-dressed Black man with defined dimples stepped to the mic.

"The Benson family wants to thank the many well-wishers and supporters of their right to claim what is rightfully theirs. Many others felt that they were wrong to request payment for what was once stolen from them by force. They wanted them to turn the cheek and let it all go. Our nation has a history of those who are powerless to remain quiet . . . to allow themselves to be bled dry and then not to ever try to request payment for their pain."

He then looked out over the crowd, those who held Black Lives Matter signs jeering at those holding Confederate flags and those wearing swastikas eye-balling those in yarmulkes. His hand tightening on the mic, he continued. "We are a divided people, but the law is the law. The Bensons have won all three lawsuits. Sarah Benson is the rightful heir to the Benson Plantation and its many business holdings. Junie Benson has won his lawsuit and reparations for his chronicled contributions to the Benson family's wealth. And the family as a whole, John, Sarah, and Junie, have won personal damages from their kidnappers, Burstein Labs and Benson Industries."

The screams and chanting of the crowd went wild. Holding up his hand, the lawyer gave one last statement. "It is our hope that the Benson family will be allowed to heal in their own time and in their own way. They ask that each and every person who is following their story give their hearts over to the love of their fellow man. Have a good day."

He then stepped away, and all the other lawyers followed him down the steps.

Unknown to the revelers, the Bensons had left through a different entrance and were already halfway home.

The Evening's Celebration . . .

Settling into the living room couch with Sari in his arms, Zachary snuggled into her neck. John growled beside them, grumbling that it was too much public affection. Junie lounged in a chair, smiling from ear to ear as he was challenged in a video game by Bebop's very cute niece. And Mother Sweat smiled at it all coming together as she knew it would.

Tapping on his Champagne flute, Zachary stood. "May I have your attention?" Everyone turned in their conversations, and the room quieted. "Dad, Mom, and the rest of my family, thank you for coming and being here through this whole ordeal. Your support has meant the world to us. Bebop, you guys are family. Thank you for always having my back. The Benson family does not trust easily, and we understand why, but they feel most secure with those in this room. This is a huge property, and with all of you coming here, we have formed our village with Bebop in the position as our sheriff."

Bebop raised his flute in a mock salute. "That title would be 'Executive Chief of Security.'"

Squeezing his hand, Sari encouraged him to continue. "Mother Sweat, you moving here too provides us with the in-house spiritual guidance we . . . well, *I* need to continue my growth now that I am a believer."

"Well, well," his mother chanted as the rest of the crowd whistled.

Zachary continued. "John gave me permission to court Sari, and in a private moment between us, she said, yes. So I'm getting my green-eyed goddess. People tend to disregard their dreams, but I'm here to tell you not to. Your dreams are a way for the Holy Spirit to speak to you when you're too hardheaded to listen."

Sari pulled him down and said, "I don't know when he started talking so much."

The group laughed in a good-natured way. Together.

"He's been my knight in shining armor, although I don't suppose little girls believe in that anymore. But forgive me; I can honestly say I'm from a different time. Zachary and I will go through premarital counseling as he joins with my family, and we continue to get healed from the ordeal of being held in bondage. We didn't know the importance of healing from trauma, but we are learning and improving. Winning our case brings some vindication. I no longer wake up in the night in cold sweats. I think my papa, my *only* father, has something to say, then Junie, as we keep this party going."

John stood, coughing among sniggers of his obvious discomfort. "I had a heap of bitterness piled mountain high, dis and dat resentment—building." Then his emotions high, he stopped.

"Take your time, baby. Tell it yo' way," Mother Sweat called out.

Inhaling, John continued. "I couldn't breathe easy from it. My heart *hurt*. Then a man named Donald, who didn't look like me, helped us. Then I met Zachary—made me rock his jaw—but he gon' be a good son. Zachary took me to meet men who was all kinds of thangs, Black, White, Hispanic, working together—brothers. I heard a man say on the television, we play checkers while God is playing three-dimensional chess. I don't think that word will ever leave me. Every person who showed me different than I knew chipped at my mountain. And I didn't even know'd it. In fear of others, we ran, but when the fear left, the healing began. I forgive so that I can live."

He then looked over at Saundra, who had been out of a job and was now the family's head of housekeeping. "I found out thirty-eight years old is pretty young, and I have a lot more of life to live." Then shyly, sharing a not-so-secret smile with Saundra, he stated firmly, "Gon' get to it."

A resounding cheer went up, and then he sat beside Saundra, thigh to thigh.

Junie stood, his spry chest puffed. "I can talk a lot, but I won't. When Burstein Lab went up in smoke, and its owner went on the run, I felt justice." Inhaling, he continued, "Escaping, we was in survival mode. We really had no other choice. It took grown folk courage when we sued the

Benson family. I want to thank everyone, including the men and women guarding the parameters of our grounds, who showed me what courage looks like."

The group burst into wild applause and cheering.

Sari called out. "So much for not talking long, Junie."

Junie giggled, then became somber. "One last thing, Sari girl. I can now freely call the voice I hear . . . the voice of God. I think I didn't feel worthy enough to name Him. Why would He pick me, make me different, single me out for such a grand adventure? He gave me a mind to learn and even in captivity, gave me the dream that we would use the courts to untangle the lies of a century." Pointing to the books lining the shelves, he said, "I read about Jefferson's descendants, who didn't receive their due. And Henrietta Lack's family, who Edgar Burstein thought to take our cells and blend with hers to make a fortune, and her people never got a dime. I hope that they know this victory is theirs. I want to thank you all for being our family. We still miss those we used to warm the hearth with, like Mama, Cinda, and Ol' Silas. We'll live this life for all of them. I'm finished now, Sari."

Cheers went up around the room, Sari's the loudest as the food and beverages flowed, and everyone enjoyed themselves. Everywhere you looked were smiles on joy-filled faces that had helped when nothing was in it for them.

Mother Sweat waved her perfumed hankie in the air and grabbed the hand of Saundra's mother, Rose. "You know, I get happy looking around. You see, everyone in this room understood Corinthians 9:10, 'He will give seed to the sower.' Peoples say when they get theirs what they're going to do for folk. But we serve an active God, and He gives seed to the *sower*. See, that's activated potential. Activated potential is someone walking toward fulfilling their purpose *now* sans excuses. And as they went forward, they sowed, no matter how much they had." She pointed at Saundra. "You're a blessing, darling, you and Saul. Called and answered." She pointed to Bebop. "And even in the face of demonic danger, sowing . . . seed. Keep sowing, y'all. There's more work ahead."

She then pointed to Bebop's son, who was playing the music. "Now, hit me with something Mother can rock her hips to." She pulled up Rose, and the two senior citizens shook their shoulders and defied gravity as they rocked their hips back and forth, down to the ground. "Aww, Sookie, Sookie, now."

People jumped up to dance, filling the room with carefree energy. Then quietly, Sari and Zachary slipped out of the room.

Perfumed flowers filled the summer evening's atmosphere. Putting his arms around her waist, Zachary danced Sari around the courtyard. Then the music changed to a Kem classic. Sari, swaying in time, her body formed to his as Zachary whispered, "We need to have this wedding soon. I'm not going to make it if we don't."

"Well, I thought a fall wedding would be nice. Just the folk here attending and our attorneys."

They continued to sway as Zachary said, "You know, a woman as young, fine, and as wealthy as you could do better."

"Sure I can." At his protest, she giggled and said, "But I want you. This two hundred million dollars is going to help an awful lot of people. And instead of this being a shrine to a past long gone, these acres will make a wonderful place for Junie's young scholar academy, and it will be free to all."

"Yes, and my new security force manned by the men and women from the compound and other displaced veterans will rescue and provide a safe place for women and children who are trafficked—a problem that is out of control."

"I love the idea that they will have ongoing, trauma-informed treatment. It's really helping all of us."

"I learned from how you have all embraced getting the help you need to heal. I'm so proud of all of you. And the way you've forgiven it all keeps me humble. It encouraged me to call Sylvia and wish her well. It didn't go well, but I'm unburdened."

"Zachary?"

"Yes, baby."

"Did you tear me away from everyone to talk to me about plans already made and work we've committed to? Or to kiss me?"

"Easy answer." Molding his lips to hers, he pulled gently on her lower lip and traced it with his tongue. He then framed her face in his large, suntanned hands and pulled her in even farther as he moved in a rhythm that caused physical tremors to snake up her body.

Gasping for air, she said, "No, not fall . . . end of summer . . . maybe even an end-of-this-month wedding."

Pulling her back into him, Zachary backed them into the wall and hit the outside light switch off. Sari gave a mewling sound. Then some rustling followed by a deep moan was heard. Zachary panted, "Next week would be better."

Junie sat on the back garden bench, now covered in darkness. He didn't mean to overhear their private conversation, but he was happy for his sister. He came out because it all got to be overwhelming. So much had happened, and there was so much more to do. Most of it would include him learning as he went. Finally, after the professors Senator Benson hired and the ones they had hired since they began working with trusted attorneys, he was almost ready to take his college entrance exams. He no longer doubted himself.

He knew when he couldn't trust man, he could trust the voice of God. Why He brought them into the new millennium, Junie didn't know. But he did know it was God that brought them here. He even used the forces of evil to awaken them safely. He also understood that God was openly righting some wrongs that had been publicly conducted for many centuries. He demonstrated that it didn't matter how long a person, policy, or law stood. If not honed in truth, it would eventually fail.

Junie rose as the sounds from Zachary and Sari became more intimate. Looking at his watch, he saw it was ten p.m., and according to Mother Sweat, it was past his bedtime. Noiselessly moving inside toward his room, he went to the window, his mind drifting back to green fields with puffs of white cotton plants folding in the wind. He raised his eyes to the moon shining clear over a home he could now claim as his own.

Finally, peace.

Somewhere in the Ivory Coast . . .

"What's taking you so long? Come to bed, woman," Edgar yelled as he reclined on the king-sized bed.

The bathroom door opened, and Carol Heathrow inched out . . . with a strong arm firmly wrapped around her neck, cutting off her air. Her eyes bulged out of their sockets as Legend crooned into her ear.

Instantly, Edgar jumped from the bed and pulled his nightstand drawer open.

"You were looking for this?" Legend said as he lifted the gun he had taken from the drawer earlier. "Look at you all scared after what you've done to other people. A man like you should be a 'G.'" Scowling, he then grunted, "I've come to collect."

"Collect? Collect *what*? The senator is dead, and the Bensons are free. What do I owe you?"

"You lied. You cheated, and then you stole. The senator made you a promise, and I was the vehicle for that promise to be kept. I've been paid and am here now to fulfill the contract."

Carol fainted as Legend threw her on the bed. Edgar ran to the door but found it locked. He put his hands up and pleaded for mercy as snot dribbled with his hysterical tears. Legend smiled and pulled out his knife. "Not everybody deserves a happily ever after. You might find this a bit uncomfortable . . ."

About the Author

Colette R. Harrell made her debut as a traditionally published author with the book, *The Devil Made Me Do It*. The book, *Later*, is her first Indie project.

She fills her days as wife, mother, grandmother, author, playwright, and story editor. She likes nothing better than a cold day, a warm blanket, and a good book.

She aims to engage readers and provide them with wisdom and humor in an entertaining way. Her biggest lesson is that it takes a village to raise a dream, and she considers each of her readers part of that village.

She would love for you to share your thoughts in a review.